what about Anna?

what about Anna?

Jan Simoen

translation by
John Nieuwenhuizen

Walker & Company
New York

First published in 1999 as En met Anna? in the Netherlands by Em Querido's Uitgeverij B.V. First English language edition published in 2001 in Australia by Allen & Unwin.
First published in the United States of America in 2002 by Walker Publishing Company, Inc.

Published simultaneously in Canada by Fitzhenry and Whiteside, Markham, Ontario L3R 4T8

Library of Congress Cataloging-in-Publication Data

Simoen, Jan, 1953–
[En met Anna? English]
What about Anna? / Jan Simoen ; translation by John Nieuwenhuizen.
p. cm.
Originally published: Amsterdam : Querido, c1999.
Summary: In Belgium in 1999, upon learning that her brother who was reported killed by a landmine in Bosnia may still be alive, sixteen-year-old Anna resents that she is the only one strong enough to try to uncover the truth.
ISBN: 0-8027-8808-4
1. Yugoslav War, 1991–1995—Juvenile fiction. [1. Yugoslav War, 1991–1995—Fiction. 2. Brothers and sisters—Fiction. 3. Grief—Fiction. 4. AIDS (Disease)—Fiction. 5. Family problems—Fiction. 6. Belgium—Fiction.] I. Nieuwenhuizen, John, tra. II. Title.
PZ7.S6015 Wh 2002
[Fic]—dc21
2002016771

Visit Walker & Company's Web site at www.walkerbooks.com

Printed in the United States of America

2 4 6 8 10 9 7 5 3 1

To Anola

And the things you can't remember
tell the things you can't forget

Tom Waits

prologue

I am Jonas . . .

I am Jonas. I am dead.

I died in 1994, of a disease that was trendy at the time.

I was on TV. I remember a couple of guys who suddenly stood by my white bed. The taller one (bad shave, open khaki jacket with lots of pockets, dirty jeans, chewing gum) stood back a bit (discreetly, he'd say), but the bulging round eye of the camera on his shoulder looked at me so rudely I had the feeling he could look straight through my nostrils into my brain, the creep. The other guy (too much after-shave, gray speckled jacket, designer specs, cell phone on his belt) came and sat uninvited on the edge of my bed, greeted me as if we'd known each other for ever, went "test, one, two" a few times, shoved a microphone under my nose as if it were a Norelco, and shouted all sorts of nonsense into my ear. I needed to act naturally, be calm and relaxed and all that. I had to ignore the camera: "That camera just doesn't exist, simply isn't there, okay? Look this way, here!" and he tapped the microphone on his left shoulder, pock, pock, pock. I stared stupidly at that left shoulder, mumbling dumb answers to dumb questions, and before I realized it, it was over. "Okay, thanks, fantastic!" shouted the trendy guy, and they were gone. And I was on TV. *Smile, you're on TV?* I didn't even think of smiling, not with those teeth of mine. But anyway, whether I wanted to or not, I was a celebrity, along with about two million others. According to that weird, inescapable logic of the mass media: Only celebrities appear on TV, but being on TV is all you need to be a celebrity.

That was in 1994, late January or early February, and in my case (and the other two millions') it was all a bit more complicated. We weren't really the stars, our disease was. And our disease had become a star because quite a few stars had been killed by it: Keith Haring, Robert Mapplethorpe, Rudolf Nureyev, Arthur Ashe, Freddie Mercury . . .

(Also—this is incidental, but not irrelevant—TV liked us because we were young and thin. TV doesn't like fat, old people. TV likes young, thin people. They're much easier to frame, apparently.)

At the end of January 1994 I was twenty-six years old, very young, that is, and I was really thin. I weighed barely sixty-six pounds. To tell you the truth, I looked like a forty-century-old mummy; a bag of bones with a bald skull. My skin was almost transparent, I had a drip in my left arm (so they could pump morphine and other treats into me, *yummy!*), a tube in my nose regularly drained blood and snot, so I could at least get a little air into me with my mouth shut (I liked keeping my mouth shut, particularly when I had visitors, because my teeth rattled in their sockets like Lego blocks in a vacuum cleaner), all my hair had fallen out, my eyebrows were gone, and lesions covered me like freckles in summer. Not a pretty sight, really, but the TV people thought . . . Anyway. And it was just as well people in their living rooms didn't get a look at my insides, because they must have looked like Chernobyl after the explosion. My lungs, my stomach, my liver, my kidneys, my intestines, my pancreas: all one great lump of misery, full of swellings, spots, pustules, secondary tumors, and bleeding wounds . . . Jesus! And I had actually registered as an organ donor, can you believe it? Only my brain still functioned fairly normally, and that was a stroke of luck. So, with my natural sense of humor, I could at least treat my visitors to the occasional cheerful, slightly cynical witticism (when my teeth were up to it), and that was a bonus. Especially for the visitors, because it wasn't always clear who was comforting whom, during visiting hours.

I had a lot of visitors. Much comfort—given and received. Heaps of flowers, fruit, and chocolates. A Guust Flater cartoon, a Mano Solo CD. Cakes, a hip flask of Johnnie Walker (Hugo, of course). A small present, a warm gesture, a supportive word. Oh yes.

Sometimes an enthusiastic shout, "Hey! Jonas! How's it going, man?" followed by a thump on my shoulder. I choked on my snot, gasped for breath, had a coughing fit.

"Oops, sorry."

"No, no, it's okay, it's okay . . ."

And it really was okay. I could see from his face that he had used up half a dozen tissues blowing his nose in the corridor, and then, with his hand on the door handle and a lump still in his throat, had practiced that breezy greeting. Above all, no crying. Absolutely not.

Sometimes it was a nervous smile, no kiss, not even a

handshake. Edge of the chair, safe distance, you never know. Long look at the ceiling. Cough. Oh, yes, greetings from . . . Time I hit the road . . .

I do understand them, you know. My visitors were okay. More than okay. Jesus, everybody but everybody came.

Amsterdam and Brussels, Louvain and New York, Antwerp and Ghent, everybody.

And the laughs! They echoed through the white corridors, louder than a hundred clowns visiting the children's ward. Louder than death. Once, my doctor unexpectedly burst into the room. Hugo hid the JW behind his back, Chris only just managed to throw her cigarette out the window, and it was suddenly very quiet.

"Hey, Jonas . . ."

"Yeah, Doc?"

"Not fair, I think."

"Um, no, Doc . . ."

"You partying away, and me not invited?"

"Oh. Oh, yes, come and join us."

He sat astride a chair, lit a strictly illegal cigar, and begged Hugo for a finger of JW.

An extremely decent guy, my doctor. Every evening, after visiting time, he dropped in. I was usually pretty down then, especially that last week. He'd stand at the foot of my bed and look at me, long and searchingly. Not like a camera, no. His look really wanted to know how I was. "Well, Doc, what do you think?" I'd say, looking at him expectantly. I was so tired. But every evening he shook his head again.

"Not yet," he said. "There's more people coming."

I shrugged. I'd had enough.

"They want to see you," he said. "And you want to see them."

I didn't believe a word of it, but I trusted him. I haven't ever trusted anyone as much as I trusted my doctor then.

"If you say so," I sighed.

And he was right.

Holsbeek, of course. Holsbeek still had to come. New York and Amsterdam and Brussels and Louvain were on their way home, and that's when the Holsbeek crowd finally came. Family, ha!

Irina came to cut my nails, and she arranged the pillows behind my back, and she zipped up the corridor to ask the nurse for a new drip, or a fresh sick bowl, or clean sheets.

And Papa. Papa came too. We had never talked much, my father and I, but suddenly he was there. And damn it, it *had* been a long time. And damn it, it was good. And Michael came, too, with Marta.

They were the ones I still wanted to see, and I saw them. And vice versa.

And then Anna came.

I hadn't really wanted to see Anna (Why? Because she was so young?), but she came anyway. She came and sat on the bed. A mass of dark brown curls, and large dark brown eyes. God, she was growing up fast.

"Hey, sis," I said. "No crying."

"Hey, brother," she said. "No dying."

And then I had to cry, of course. (So *that's* why I hadn't wanted to see her.)

She was nearly eleven. Tall girl. I told her some trivial story, rattled my teeth, and she laughed through her tears. Brave girl.

Then she left, and it was time. Really time. After visiting hours, my doctor came and stood by the foot of my bed.

"Hey, Doc," I said, and he nodded. At last.

It was time.

It's not so bad, you know. Nothing special, really.

In a flash I thought of all the things I was going to have to do without: the swing in Grandma's hall, pizza from Rico on the corner of Fifth and Forty-second, a Sunday morning in Central Park, a field of wheat in Settignano, a bootleg tape of the John Lennon concert in Madison Square Garden, the foaming wake of the Dover ferry in the Ostend harbor, Susan's eyes . . . but now all that was no longer so important. Clouds moved in front of the sun, but a west wind drove them on, and suddenly I was hardly missing anything. It passed, and it passed quickly, I was lucky. The difference between being dead and not being dead is what you miss. When you're dead, you miss almost nothing anymore.

Almost.

Anna, for instance. I still miss Anna. Why her especially? I'm not sure. Because she still has to become something, that's how I think of it. She's sixteen now. Sometimes, I'd love to write to her. But that's not possible. I can't do it.

Someone else, perhaps? Hugo, for instance?

travel
phobia

Anna

Fifteen minutes earlier

All in all, that Thursday, June 17, began like a pretty normal day. It just began a bit earlier than usual. Fifteen minutes, to be precise. As usual, I got up, had a shower, ate Fruit'n'Fibre for breakfast, checked my diary (Had I prepared for the right exam? You never know), and put an apple in my school bag. A green one, as usual.

Except I did everything fifteen minutes earlier. I sometimes think those fifteen minutes caused it all, but of course that's nonsense.

I picked up my bag and shouted in the direction of the bathroom, "Mom, I'm off!"

She shouted back over the noise of her hair dryer, "Why so early?"

I knew exactly why so early but didn't feel like explaining just then, because it would've made me lose my fifteen-minute lead, so I said nothing. And while I was saying nothing, suddenly the hair dryer was silent, too.

"Hey, that's strange," she said.

"What is, Mom?"

"I was just about to switch it off, but it stopped all by itself."

"What?"

"Could you try the light, Anna?"

I flicked the switch in the hall a few times: nothing.

"Have we blown the fuses? Or is there a blackout? Or maybe it's the hair dryer, what do you think?" My mother was scared of electricity.

"Mom, I really have to go, right now!"

"Hey, hang on! What am I supposed to do? What about my hair?"

"Just wait a bit."

"Do you think so?"

Then the power was back. The hall light came on, the hair dryer roared and in my room the clock radio started blaring full blast: "Believe," by Cher, the walking face-lift. My mother screamed; I burst out laughing and switched the hall light off.

"Bye, Mom. See you this afternoon!"

"Oh, Anna! Wait, wait!"

I turned back, my hand on the doorknob.

"What would you like for lunch?"

"Doesn't matter. Just something cold. A salad or something."

"Good luck with your math!" she shouted after me.

She's a darling. She'd been taking half days off especially for my final exams, so she could spoil me. Easy enough to organize at work, she insisted. (What do you mean, Mom, easy enough? You never used to be able to manage, and now suddenly it's easy? But she said something about flexible working hours, and—raising her voice—that it had nothing, but absolutely nothing, to do with Dad, do you understand? Yes, sure, I had muttered. It was fine with me.)

I checked my watch. Nearly twenty to eight. I'd better hurry, or I'd lose my fifteen-minute advantage. Bert would be waiting for me outside the gas station at quarter to eight, so we could ride the rest of the way to school together, as usual. But today things weren't as usual. Today it was off between us, had been since yesterday. "But why?" he'd ask, and I'd reply that I didn't know, and he'd say, "I don't believe that." And that he wouldn't give up hope and so on. Boys who wouldn't believe me and hoped for a lot—it was a familiar story. That's what those fifteen minutes were about. Ridiculous, Anna.

But that's when things started. At the gas station (no Bert, phew!) one of those loud sports cars with an I Love Sex bumper sticker was filling up, "Believe" blasting from its radio. What a coincidence. Oh, well. I turned the corner and realized what had probably caused our power failure: the whole street had been dug up. Men in orange overalls swarmed all over the place with drills and shovels; piles of soil and clouds of dust were everywhere. Probably hit a cable or something. One of those men in orange, a Kurd or a Turk, I thought, waved at me. He called out something in a foreign language, and immediately I knew where he was from, because I could understand. "Dovidenja!" I shouted back, and he laughed in surprise. I was just as surprised. I hadn't managed to utter a Serbo-Croatian word for years.

Then, suddenly, as I swerved to avoid a dead hedgehog on the bike path, my front wheel skidded and I fell. At that instant, in the front garden to my right, a little boy fell off a swing. The seat swung back and hit his head with a dull thud. He started crying, but was drowned out by the screaming siren of an ambulance. For a moment it seemed as if the ambulance was coming for that little boy (already?), but it passed by, howling, and while I was scrambling up, I glimpsed its number plate: ABA 153. I rode on, and the next two cars that passed me had ABB and ABC number plates. Well, I thought. Next, every traffic light I came to changed to green, and after the third green light I discovered that my elbow was bleeding. On the corner of Acacia Avenue there was a sign, for a new shoe shop, with huge letters forming the name of my math teacher. (We did have math today, didn't we? Yes, we had math.) I tried to lick the blood off my elbow without stopping, but couldn't get at it.

Then, within one-hundredth of a second of each other, Kristel and I rode through the school gate. I frowned, because we'd never managed to do that, but then I realized she usually leaves fifteen minutes earlier than me, so it made sense. Yes, it did. She was humming "Believe" (of course!) and I wanted to ask what made her think of that song, but she shouted, "Hey, you're bleeding!" and gave me a tissue. "Truly weird, Ann!" (Kristel always calls me Ann. I don't mind that, I don't like Anna.) "I was dreaming that my grandmother was dying and then I woke up and they were playing that song on the radio, 'Believe.'" She started humming again. I was busy with the tissue; the blood from my elbow kept dripping, and I was about to ask her for another tissue when she suddenly grabbed my shoulder. That was a bit sore, too.

"And Ann, do you know what was really weird? At that very second the phone rang. It was the hospital; my grandmother had actually died."

I pressed the tissue to my mouth. "Oh, no," I said, but she turned and took off. I stood there, totally confused. I inspected my elbow. The bleeding had stopped, and I felt as if I'd just woken from a deep sleep full of dreams.

I began to realize that this was not a normal day. I spat out a piece of tissue that had stuck to my lip, locked my bike, and walked to the exam room.

When I emerged three hours later, I couldn't remember the number of my bike lock.

"Mine's 237," said Kristel.

Completely taken aback, I remembered mine was 732. Hey, thanks, I wanted to say, but Kristel rattled on before I could open my mouth.

"All morning I've been wondering what that song's got to do with it," she said.

Song? What song?

"'Believe,' of course!" she said crossly. "With my dream and my grandmother! Don't you ever understand anything?" She shrugged, rubbed something out of her eye, and was gone.

I got on my bike, caught three green lights in a row again, and passed the front garden where the little boy was sitting happily on his swing as if nothing had happened, but the dead hedgehog on the bike path was gone. I thought about Kristel and her grandmother. The men in orange were having lunch, the pneumatic drills were silent. I looked for the man who had waved at me, but couldn't see him—and suddenly Bert was riding behind me.

Oh, no, I thought, not now, not today. So I ignored all my feelings of regret and started pedaling faster. Poor Bert. The umpteenth boyfriend, but definitely the nicest. Perhaps even the Right Boy, but wrong time, wrong place, as always. I couldn't help it, and he couldn't understand at all. I could sympathize with that, especially today. He followed me for a little while but turned left at the service station. When I turned into our street, I was alone between the hot rows of houses.

I slammed the front door pretty hard, and my mother called out from the kitchen.

"Is that you, Anna?"

Of course it was me, who else would it be? There wasn't anybody else anymore, not in this street, not in this house. I shouted something back and walked straight through to the garden. And for the first time that day, walking into the garden, I felt I belonged somewhere. I breathed deeply.

She had set the table under the cherry tree, and it looked like paradise. My mother was great at creating atmosphere: the cane chairs, the white tablecloth, the glass salad bowl, the bottles, the glasses—even the dappled shadow from the leaves of the tree—it was as if she'd laid it all on especially for me. For a second I had the feeling I'd walked into an advertisement for olive oil or low-cholesterol margarine, but at the same time I knew how real all this was, and it somehow made me think of the past.

It nearly made me cry.

I sank into one of the cane chairs, shut my eyes, and tried to think about that knot in my stomach. Why was I so tense? Wasn't everything going well for me? I was doing okay in my exams, my mother loved me, my father too, in his own way; I had heaps of friends, the weather was lovely, and the longest holiday of my life was about to begin. Of course, there was Bert—I'd broken up with him again, but that was nothing new. Boys who kept hoping against all the evidence, a drag, but . . .

But what about those omens? Those coincidences? Normally I wouldn't take any notice of that sort of nonsense. I was a levelheaded girl, quite experienced in many ways . . . but I have to admit I was feeling anxious. It felt as if today could have been the last "normal" day of my life.

I pulled myself together. Been watching too many soaps, Anna? *She suddenly realized her life would never be the same again* . . . Ridiculous. And yet . . .

It was almost unnaturally still. Not a leaf stirred. Shreds of memory wafted over me. Grandma, the swing in the hall, Dad, Jonas, Michael, voices from New York, ex-Yugoslavia, Bosnia, refugees. I tried to chase them away, but they kept drifting back like flies.

Then a balmy little breeze blew up, brushing gently against my throat, my ears, my neck. It moved softly along my spine, under my T-shirt. I shivered. I breathed deeply through my nose and smelled the scent of fresh basil.

And then I heard her voice. Mama? Mom? Is that you?

"Hey, is something the matter?"

I looked up. My mother was standing in front of me, looking at me searchingly, almost like a doctor. She was carrying a bowl of tomatoes and mozzarella. Smiling, I shook my head and stretched.

"Just tired."

She put the bowl on the table, ran her fingers through my hair, and sat down opposite me.

"It's getting long again," she said.

"What's getting long?"

"Your hair. Are you growing it again?"

"I might."

I sat up straight, drawing my fingers through my dark brown curls. They felt as if they'd been cut with a pair of hedge clippers. Suddenly I noticed how good she looked. Had for a couple of months, really. A sort of sharpness in her face, just enough gray in that thick black hair of hers (I had inherited my curls from her), and with that hint of sadness in her eyes that made them look warm, as if her grief for Michael had settled.

At last, I thought, at long last. After nearly three years, it was about time.

I wondered if all that had anything to do with Dad's leaving. Perhaps you needed to be alone for certain kinds of sorrow. But why was I wondering about that, today of all days?

"Aren't you eating?" she asked.

"Yes, I am, of course. It's lovely."

I filled my plate. Milky white mozzarella. Fresh basil on

the tomatoes. During the last few months my mother had been growing herbs in a bed by the garden wall.

"Well, eat then."

"Okay, okay." I started eating, but she didn't. "What's wrong?" I asked, my fork full of mozzarella.

"I like to see it long. You've got such lovely hair. But I shouldn't be saying that, of course."

"No."

A quick smile from me, a shy smile from her. For a moment, there was silence. There was so much I wouldn't let her say, so, with an inviting smile, I granted her two questions: one of the "mother-daughter" kind (something about my exam), one "just-us-girls-together" (something about my boyfriends).

"Ask away," I said, my mouth full.

"How did the math go?"

"Awful, of course."

Strictly according to the rules, I said it as curtly and pessimistically as possible, and we both burst out laughing. She knocked over her glass of white wine, jumped up, giggling, to save her trousers, and for a moment, just for a moment, there under the cherry tree, we were really close, really mother-and-grown-up-daughter-together. We gasped for breath, laughing, and already I was getting ready for the next question, the one about the boyfriends. Sure enough, she leaned toward me conspiratorially and whispered, "Well, have you given him the push?"

"Who?"

"Come on, Anna . . ." She nudged me. Girls together.

"Oh, Bert? Number seventeen, you mean?"

More giggles, more laughing, but now it was really getting too close, under that cherry tree, and after another fit of laughter our conversation faltered, like an engine that's run out of fuel.

"Ah . . ." she said, rubbing the tears from her eyes.

"Mom?"

"Yes?"

I opened my mouth to tell her something about today, about all those weird omens, but she suddenly gave me a look I didn't like. A look from the past. The thought flashed through my mind, From here on, this conversation can only be about things I don't like. And in some way or other, I knew she was aware of it, too. The way she was looking at me.

"Never mind," I said.

She sniffed. "Dad's going to ring you later, around two."

There it was! But I said, "Okay," and shrugged. She was silent. I pushed my chair aside a bit, because the sun had moved on and I wanted shade.

"You're growing up," she said.

"Oh, Mom, please!"

"It's true, though, isn't it? Your last exam tomorrow. The end of school."

Yes, sure, I nodded, resigned.

"Well, yes, then it starts, doesn't it? I mean, everything . . . you'll go to college, live on your own. . . . It's all gone so fast. . . . It seems only yesterday that I was singing to you. . . . Lullabies . . . but you wouldn't remember . . ."

"Oh, yes, I do. In Serbo-Croatian."

Her sad smile was back, and that strange frown. Once . . .

No, not now, I decided. I got up, my skirt sticking to my thighs. I went over to her, grabbed her thick hair, and planted a kiss on it. "I'm going now," I wanted to say, because I had decided—weird day or not, omens or no omens—I was really going to study for that last exam. Suddenly she turned her face to me, squinting.

"How strange," she said, passing her hands over her eyes, as if she wanted to wipe something away. I knew what it was.

"What, Mom? What's strange?"

"Jonas used to . . ."

As I had thought: Jonas.

"Mom? Please. I've got an exam tomorrow. I really want to . . ."

"Of course, off you go, darling. I'm sorry."

But I stayed where I was. "Come on then, tell me."

She gave me a quick glance, pursed her lips, and pretended to think. "Well . . . One day Jonas kissed me in exactly that way. He grabbed my hair—it wasn't gray yet, oh well, perhaps a tiny bit—and kissed it. Exactly the way you did then. That's all. It suddenly reminded me."

Jonas, my big brother, my spitting image. Was I always going to be just like him?

"When was that?"

But she brushed the past aside. Reluctantly, I could see, but I didn't insist.

"I'm off," I said.

She nodded, but I wasn't even halfway up the stairs when she called after me. "Oh, Anna, there's a letter for you."

I suddenly felt cold. My hand froze on the banister, and I thought: This is it. This had to be it. The omens. This weird day.

The ancient Romans read the future in the flight of birds. Or they cut open dogs and read it in the entrails. Siberian shamans saw the future in rising smoke. Kristel's gran was dead, the number plates were ABA, ABB, and ABC, and the number of my bike lock was 732. More than five million copies of "Believe" had been sold, they said on MTV. My lips were moving, saying, "Dovidenja."

Her life would never be the same again . . .

I turned around as if in slow motion. "Why didn't you tell me before?"

Silence.

"Mom, why?"

"It's in the hall, next to the phone."

"Thanks."

I instantly recognized the handwriting on the envelope. I looked over my shoulder, looking for someone who wasn't there. She sat in the garden, thinking about the past. *Dovidenja.*

Hugo Vandamme. So *that* was it. Today of all days he had to write to me, after those years of silence.

But where was this guy hanging out? I couldn't read the postmark, and kept staring at those three strange stamps on the envelope. Little churches in sunny mountain landscapes.

Republika Hrvatska. Croatia? Yugoslavia? (Correction: ex-Yugoslavia?)

"Istria!" my mother called from the garden. She was back.

"What did you say, Mom?"

"Istria! That's where that letter's from! The Dalmatian coast!"

I looked back at the envelope. One of the stamps said "Rovinj." Tapping the edge of the envelope with my fingernail, I tried to think, but too many thoughts were crowding my brain. Hugo Vandamme had written to me, he of all people, from ex-what's-it of all places, and his letter arrived today. Today of all days. I felt as if a swing had hit me in the head.

Was that it? It was, I could feel it.

I heard quick steps in the hall, the clatter of plates and cutlery, the fridge opening and closing. All of it far too loud.

"Mom, do you know that place, Rovinj?"

"Yes, I've been there once, when I was little, with my parents. It's one of those holiday spots, you know, typical fishing village. They used to have some sort of summer festival, I think, music, theater, that sort of thing."

It all came out in a rush, as if she'd rehearsed it. Of course she'd had just as much of a shock as me when she recognized Hugo's handwriting.

A music festival, of course. Hugo was a music promoter. For some sort of cultural center in Brussels.

"Mom, does it still exist, that festival in—what was it?"

"Rovinj? I don't know. I haven't been there since the war."

She turned the tap on full, water rushed, and she started

washing up. She rattled the dishes noisily. Yugoslavia after the war—that other war—it was still a sensitive topic. And immediately I realized why she had been reminded of Jonas. Hugo was Jonas's closest friend. Used to be. And Michael's. Once.

"Will you tell me what he says?" she called over the din of the dishes.

"Who?"

I went to the kitchen, leaned against the door frame. I could see her shoulder blades moving angrily under her thin blouse.

"Come on, Anna! I know his handwriting perfectly well. Hugo used to write to us so often." She looked at me over her shoulder. "To us once, now he writes to *you*. That's how it goes."

"Oh, Mom!"

"It's all right," she said gently. "But when you write back, give him my best."

"Okay."

This time, I went to the top of the stairs and shut the door of my room. June 17, half past one in the afternoon. I went to the window and drew back the curtain. The sky was an immaculate blue; it was a peaceful day, apart from that one little Yugoslavia-cloud. And those omens—yes, those too.

I let my eyes move over the back of the big apartment block on Fontein Street, three gardens along. Nearly all the sunshades were down, and there probably wasn't anybody home this time of the day. Only the poodle belonging in 6B (occupant: solitary elderly man, probably a widower) was asleep on the balcony.

I shut the curtain, threw the letter onto my desk, took my T-shirt off, and lay down on the bed. There were cobwebs hanging from the ceiling. The day was getting hotter.

Hugo

I hesitated for a long time

I hesitated for a long time before I sent Anna that letter, and I'm still not sure if it was such a good idea. Strange, I'm not normally a hesitating sort of person.

Hesitant. What a peculiar word. Only recently, unwinding slowly in an all-night bar in Munich, I tried to explain to a saxophonist from Surinam that *hesitant* has a special meaning where I come from. It's used to describe a bed. A particular kind of bed, of course, with a mattress somewhere between thirty-nine and forty-seven inches wide. Too wide for a single person, not wide enough for a couple, unless that couple is terribly in love. And that sort of love never lasts long, I said to this guy from Surinam, and he nodded thoughtfully. "Love is like a stove," he said. "It burns you when it's hot," which wasn't particularly original, since it's from a song by Gram Parsons. Then he ordered another two Bacardi Breezers. I hate Bacardi Breezers. They remind me of Burt Bacharach.

And I hate hesitant people. I'm not a hesitant person. Bloody hell.

Just ask people who think they know me well—and there are plenty—if they would describe me that way. Hugo Vandamme, *hesitant?* Come on, they'll say, and proceed to describe me as an adventurous, funny, sharp, unpredictable, socially adept, and particularly resilient young man, with a fantastically good nose for everything that's new but not quite cool (but will be soon). And they'll go on to explain that I'm a shrewd negotiator, musically well educated, that I can draw on a good measure of natural charm, as well as maintaining an excellent relationship with Brother Alcohol, which has been invaluable in making contacts in the world of music.

Music often floats on alcohol, and I'm addicted to music.

In short, I am the right man in the right place: the perfect music promoter, on the reasonably generous payroll of a not insignificant cultural center in the capital of Europe.

And I'm fast. In this trade, you're either fast or you're dead. A brilliant new accordionist in Chechnya, a *djembé* player who is suddenly all the rage on the Ivory Coast, a grunge band in Antwerp, a rising hip-hop star in Liverpool, a charismatic singer from the Nile Delta? I've barely heard about it, and I'm on the plane rushing there. I look, I listen, and I decide, and if all goes well, they're playing in Brussels in two months (and often the talk of the town two weeks later). "Hugo? He's fast," Marc Ribot once said about me, and a month later he was playing guitar on Tom Waits's new CD.

Hesitate? Me? Not often. Until recently, that is.

Early in May I got invited to a music festival in Rovinj. Rovinj? Where the hell is Rovinj? Istria? Oh, right, Istria. What in God's name is Istria? It vaguely reminded me of something, but never mind. The festival program was certainly very interesting. A kind of new postwar ethno-techno music seemed to have evolved in the area, and the accompanying tape sounded promising. Badly recorded, lots of hiss and crackle, but very in-your-face, full-on, wham-bang stuff, totally out of control, but intelligent, too. As I listened, I even started swinging. Karen had her hand on the phone ready to book me a flight when, suddenly, paralysis struck. Total paralysis. I pressed stop, and an unreal silence hit the office. Everyone was looking at me (I thought). "Don't worry about it," I said to Karen. "I'm not going." The people at work—who thought they knew me well—couldn't understand it. I had to be ill. So I went through the motions of making a doctor's appointment, which I didn't keep. I booked a few flights myself, which I deliberately missed. I behaved as if suddenly Brussels couldn't do without me. Important meetings of the Inner City Renewal Working Party, you know. People at work shook their heads. What's the matter with Hugo?

Eventually I actually left—I couldn't avoid it any longer. It was only when the letters CRO lit up next to my flight number on the departures board that the reason for all this hesitation became clear. (How deeply can one repress something? —*A man can have the illusion that he understands everything, except his own shadow.* Lao Tse.)

It was the region, of course. Istria was Croatia, and Croatia, that was ex-Yugoslavia, and ex-Yugoslavia meant Michael. For years I had managed to zap ex-Y off the screen of my mind, but now the batteries in my remote control were flat, and I was stuck on that program. I had to keep watching. Oh, Michael.

Michael was my closest friend when we were at Louvain University. I took sinology (an impulse), Michael musicology (the real vocation). Music brought us together. I was better at talking about it, but Michael was at least ten times more musical than me. My God, what a musician! If I was Colonel Parker, then he was the young Elvis. He played the clarinet exquisitely, and his great love was Béla Bartók, a Romanian-Hungarian composer. A guy from the Balkans, just like Michael. I couldn't understand the Balkans at all, but I loved Michael.

The Balkans, God damn it. Halfway through his studies, when he was in Italy on a scholarship, war broke out in the bloody Balkans. Romania, from memory. Ceausescu, that's when it all started. He felt involved.

"I have to go there, Hugo," he said. It was the few days of the Christmas holidays in Louvain, and we were drinking Duvel beer in our favorite pub, which was in a bit of a sad state, really. They played new beat music, and the waiters wore T-shirts with bow ties printed on them. December 1989 that was, the Berlin Wall had just come down, and he'd been in Berlin when it happened. (Michael was a bit like me that way: he always had to be there.)

"Ah, my friend," I said, "let those bastards smash each other's heads in. You concentrate on your music. What on earth have you got to do with those fire-eaters? You're not a nationalist, are you? You hate nationalists!"

"My father lives there," he said.

Oops. Forgot. Michael's father was a Croatian. Or a Serb. Or something in between. Anyway, a Yugoslav.

"But I thought you'd lost touch with your father? I mean, how long have you lived here now, you and Irina, um, your mother?"

"A long time. Seven, eight years. But my parents had already separated in '76 or '77."

"And in all that time—?"

"Not a sign of life. . . . Just as well. After the separation, my mother's greatest fear was that he'd turn up one day."

"So?"

He sighed. "Listen, Vandamme, my father's a bastard. Or, anyway, he was a bastard fourteen years ago, and I've no reason to believe he's changed the slightest bit. Macho, tyrannical, a rabid nationalist, and a professional soldier on top of that. Even when Tito was still alive, he kept going on about Greater Serbia." (Ah, a Serb.) "I still can't imagine how my mother ever got married to him."

"She was pregnant, you told me once."

"With me, yes, I know."

"And your mother is . . . ?" I had forgotten again, to my shame.

"Croatian," Michael said patiently. "We lived in Croatia, too. I was born in Split."

"Split," I mused. "A prophetic name."

He laughed briefly, with a hiccup. "The perfect city for a separation, yes."

"So, if I understand, you're half-Croatian, half-Serb."

"Officially, I'm half-Belgian, half-Yugoslav. Croatia is still not officially a country. But my name is Serbian: Lupovic."

I tapped my temple with my index finger. "And your father is a freaked-out full-blooded Serb who, if you ever bump into him, will address you with a bazooka rather than with words, because you're a dirty bastard with unclean blood and besides you are, in embryonic form, the cause of his wretched marriage to a Croatian slut—"

"Mind your language, Vandamme! You're talking about my mother here!"

"I'm quoting, my friend, I'm quoting!"

He sat down, but his eyes were fiery.

Beware the sleeping volcano, said the divine Lao Tse. Cautiously, I finished my argument. "Michael, my friend, once more: What do you want to go there for? What in God's name does that nationalistic madness mean to you? You're one of the least prejudiced, most broad-minded, peace-loving people I know. Please, amigo, don't come and tell me it's your blood? Blood and soil? Surely not, Michael?"

But suddenly his eyes became very sad. He called the waiter and ordered more Duvel, although he usually treats Brother Alcohol with suspicion.

"Hey, Michael?" I muttered.

"There's more," he said, and then sighed. "Ah, Vandamme . . . ," trailing three dots after my name, and I suddenly knew what it was. I straightened my back and looked him hard in the eyes.

"What's her name?"

He smiled sadly. Bingo!

"Marta," he said, adding that she was the most beautiful girl in the world, and she came from Slovenia (Slovenia was another piece of Yugoslavia, soon to become ex-Yugoslavia), and that in his country, or rather her country—well, that no-country—all sorts of craziness was about to happen, war and so on, and that he had never seen a girl like her before. Bloody hell, Vandamme, bloody hell, what was he going to do, what was he going to do? And then there was his father mixed up in it somehow. He couldn't make sense of it, he was totally confused. He couldn't bloody well sit and stare at his stupid music in bloody sunny Italy and be madly in love while in his, her, country a bloody war was about to break out?

"Mmm . . . no," I muttered. I'd never known Michael to swear so much, but his message got through. I understood Michael, he felt I understood him, and we talked for hours about beautiful girls and ex-countries and ex-fathers and roots and about blood being thicker than water—in a word, about blood in that sense.

June 8, 1999, and flight SN745 took me almost soundlessly to Istria, Croatia, former Yugoslavia, while I thought about Michael.

Three years earlier, in October 1996, my friend Michael and his Marta had disappeared in that ex-country of his (where his father also lived). On a United Nations mission: They both worked for UNICEF.

All we heard about it here, in our safe western world, was a very brief, businesslike message from the International Red Cross. Their Land Rover had hit a mine, somewhere in Bosnia, near the border town of Foca. (What, for God's sake, is a border? Never quite worked that out.) Four charred bodies were found in the totally burned-out vehicle: two military, two civilians. The two military were identified as Louis Castenac and Yannick Queffelec, of French nationality, members of a SFOR demining team. The two civilians, a man and a woman, "could not be identified with certainty. Most likely they were Michael Lupovic and Marta Ugresic, who were known to have gotten into the Land Rover that morning, October 3, 1996." Our world-famous State Police identification team obviously wasn't yet operational at the time.

"Could not be identified with certainty." For a time I had clung to that phrase, like a drowning man to a piece of driftwood. Was that cowardly? I don't know. I repeated the phrase to Irina on one of my visits to Holsbeek. "In a war the strangest things can happen, Irina. You never know. . . ." To bolster her courage, I suppose. She nodded gratefully, and set off on a trip. On a search, against her own better judgment. I was there when she got back a few weeks later, exhausted, empty. The three of us sat around the kitchen table in the middle of the night—Anna had long since gone to bed—and Pierre, her second husband, said to her, "You must forget, Irina, there's no point. We have to learn to live with the dead." The dead. Plural. Of course: first Jonas, and now Michael.

And again I nodded, cowardly, like some guy on the sidelines. Yes, of course, we had to learn to live with it.

And ever since, "forget" had been the order of the day. Try to forget. Learn to live with the dead. Forget the dead. My visits to Holsbeek became even more infrequent, and then I got a letter from Anna. "*Please*, Hugo, don't ever write to me again." And I had enjoyed writing to her so much.

Rovinj was as beautiful as a travel brochure: the sea the deepest blue, the sky the lightest blue, the hotel three-star, the waiters arrogant and ill-tempered. It was almost like Nice or Paris. Had a war raged here? Mortar bombs, Kalashnikovs, low-flying MiGs? Burning houses, smoking ruins, mutilated corpses, streams of ragged refugees? Milosevic?

"Not here, sir. In Zagreb three days. In Dubrovnik it was more, of course," a slightly less arrogant waiter told me. He was a bit older, in his mid-fifties, I guessed.

Ah, yes, I nodded, relieved. Yes, yes, of course, in Dubrovnik it was more, of course. . . . Oh, Dubrovnik, yes, I knew all about that. Seen it live on TV, zapping from MTV to CNN.

"But my son, he was in the army. He was killed by the Serbs. He was twenty-two."

I choked on my gin and tonic, quickly put my sunglasses on, pretending to admire the clear blue sea and the deep blue sky, etc. The war was everywhere here, even if you couldn't see it. I gave the waiter a big tip, and he looked at me as if I'd made a contribution to his son's funeral. Or did I imagine that? Whatever. I decided I'd better get to work.

The next two days I went to concerts, made contacts, hung out with musicians in the bar, and kept my ear to the ground, looking for new trends and interesting contracts, all that sort of rubbish. And then it happened.

It was at an open-air concert by a local band (the one on the cassette), a kind of ethno-techno affair, a mix of live music and electronics (or a combination of folk and hip-hop, you name it). On the stage were a row of guys in black leather pants, with shaved heads and bare torsos, complete with drums and torches—an ironic response to growing neo-fascism, it seemed to me, fairly controversial, but musically not uninteresting, no, definitely not uninteresting. Anyway, I stood there swaying with the crowd a bit in a professionally-detached-but-involved-as-well way, when a lightning flash hit me. No more than two yards away, I saw a blond head of hair. Very long, very blond. Flaxen. Oh no, I thought, this can't be, this can't be. Red Cross telexes flashed through my mind—"Land Rover hits land mine"—but this was . . . Oh yes, this was her, it couldn't be anyone else. There could only be one head as blond, as flaxen blond, as that. I forced my way through the crowd, grabbed her shoulder, she turned, and—yes, oh God, yes, it was her!

Marta. Michael's Marta.

She recognized me instantly. The drums on the stage were hitting my eardrums like mortar bombs, but we recognized each other, and the next instant we were hugging madly, and it was as if death itself had died.

What happened next? Oh, I don't know. I still don't.

She disappeared, she just disappeared again, floated away in a sea of people. And Michael? No, to be honest, Michael I haven't found yet. But he's alive, I know that for sure. No doubt about that.

Plenty of other doubts. Doubting Vandamme, God damn it. Should I write to someone? And if so, to whom? Pierre? Irina? Out of the question. False hope is worse than no hope. That left Anna. God knows how long I hesitated before I did write. And was that the right decision? I don't know that either.

We had agreed, Anna and I. But these were circumstances beyond my control. And anyway, Anna's now sixteen, almost an adult. Anna's pretty tough. But Anna's scared, too, I know. Scared of the memory. And I understand, oh yes. Memory can do weird things. *If you really want to remember something, try to forget it,* said the divine Lao Tse, and who am I to contradict him?

The letter

Listen, little monster

Rovinj, June 10, 199?

Dear Anna,

Haven't heard from you for a long time. Well, you haven't heard from me either. By the way, Happy birthday! (June 12, isn't it? I owe you sixteen roses. White ones.)

Listen, little monster, I've got some weird news for you, and I'm going to totally ignore our agreement. Sincere apologies, but this is an emergency.

My news comes from Rovinj, a picturesque little coastal town in Istria (Croatia, right?). Popular holiday spot, typical fishing village, fourteenth-century walls and a cathedral with two stars in the Michelin Guide.

To kick off the tourist season they have an annual music festival, and that's what I'm here for. Last night I was at a hot concert by some local celebrities (sort of techno-ethnic tough guys with bare torsos and tight leather pants, big drums, flaming torches, and clouds of smoke, but a lot of fun and a wild crowd). I was rocking along with the crowd when I suddenly became aware of a girl with long flaxen hair—girl, I said, but a middle-aged woman to you, I suppose. About thirty, I mean.

Anyway, seeing her gave me a shock, and I started to struggle through the crush toward her. I grabbed her by the shoulder. She turned and looked me straight in the eyes. I hadn't been wrong.

Anna, when you read this, you'll be as shocked as she and I were. It was Marta. Michael's Marta. Marta, honestly.

She recognized me instantly. She clamped her hand over her mouth, shaking her head. Then she threw herself in my arms. Seconds, centuries later, she broke free and looked at me again, but first she had to wipe the tears from her eyes. So did I, to be honest. I bent toward her, shouting in her ear that she was as lovely as ever (which I meant) and some more of that sort of heartwarming nonsense (you know me). She shouted a few things in my ear, too, but I could only catch the odd phrase, because the boys on stage were banging their drums louder and louder, so we ended up standing there nodding and looking at each other rather foolishly.

Then I shouted, "What about Michael?" She raised her thumb, but immediately her face clouded over and she pointed at her ears.

I thought she hadn't heard me properly, so I bent as close as I could to her ear and shouted even louder, "What about Michael?"

She clutched at my arms and shouted into my ear so loudly it hurt, "Okay!" Again, a cloud came over her face and she pointed at her ears.

Have to get away from here, I thought, somewhere quieter where we can talk at normal volume. But just as I was about to grab her by the arm so we could escape from this madness, the heroic drummers on stage broke into some sort of local top hit. The crowd began to surge, shouting, and suddenly she had disappeared. I tried all sorts of maneuvers, but Marta had gone, swallowed up by the seething waves of people. I felt like a piece of wreckage adrift. I'll spare you the details, but my night ended in a grubby little café where I made friends, in a very hazy way, with a couple of local accordion players, and briefly thought I'd dreamt it all.

But this morning in my hotel room I pinched my arm hard a few times, took a mega dose of fizzy aspirin, and remembered everything. Razor-sharp.

Then I started a search. I asked questions in a dozen or so hotels, even went to the town hall as well as the Belgian consulate, but found no sign of Marta Ugresic anywhere. Still, I am absolutely certain: *Marta was here!*

Anna, my dearest little monster, I don't dare tell your parents about this. Not yet. (Red felt pen? Censorship? I'm afraid so!)

I know your mother was here, here in Croatia, to search for Michael (and/or Marta). She's tried everything, searched everywhere. I was staying with you in Holsbeek when your father—nearly three years ago now—told your mother she had to let it go. "There's no point, Irina," he said. "Bury the past. We have to learn to live with the dead."

That's why I don't dare say anything to them now. Not yet.

But I think he's alive. I wasn't mistaken, Anna. I recognized Marta, and she recognized me (sorry to be so repetitive, but I have to convince myself and write it down again). And when I asked about Michael, she raised her thumb and said, "Okay." That can mean only one thing, can't it? That he's alive and well. Or don't I get it?

Listen, Anna, we haven't written to each other for a long time, but now I think we have to. Or better still, you and I should have a long *talk*. You and I, yes, because we can't let your parents in on this. Not yet. There is almost nothing to go on.

Tonight I'm leaving for Belgium, with a brief stop in Vienna. From June 18 to July 12 I'm on the coast, for the Sunset Festival. (Come and visit me there. Get onto www.sunsetfestival.com for addresses, etc.) Perhaps I'll know more then . . .

It doesn't happen to me often, little monster, but I'm completely confused. Full of doubts. What should we do about this? I think you're the best person to give this past some sort of future. Do something, Anna, and let me know soon.

Love,
Hugo

PS. Sorry again about the red felt pen.

Anna

My eye was furious

Ever got a letter like that? I haven't either.

I had to read it four times before the words began to register.

I sat at my desk and felt every single separate drop of sweat breaking out of every single separate pore of my high forehead. Too high, that forehead. Too many drops. I sat motionless until a drop ran into my eye, making it water. Then my left hand moved. It wiped the sweat and tears out of my eye. My eye was furious.

Merde, Hugo, what are you doing to me?

Should I be happy? Happy and excited, storming down the stairs, waving the letter like a winning lottery ticket? "Mom, read this! Michael's alive! He's alive! Hallelujah!"

No way. Strictly *verboten*. Red felt pen. (Where had I heard that before? It had something to do with Jonas, I thought.) That's why I don't dare tell them anything now. Not yet.

You're a coward, Hugo! Doing this to me, how dare you, man! Telling me so much, and then punishing me by forcing this never-ending secrecy onto me!

And why me? Why do this to me of all people? Silly little sixteen-year-old me?

. . . to give this past some sort of future.

Bullshit, Vandamme! Social workers' talk! Half-baked

rubbish! Maybe Michael had a talent for saving the world, but I don't, do you hear, I don't! For God's sake let the dead stay dead!

Mom is just about all right, with her grief in some sort of perspective. So for heaven's sake don't turn up with such a crazy little sparkle of hope! Leave me in peace, man! I was just doing so well. Yeah, reasonably well.

What's that you said, Hugo? A sparkle of hope is better than no hope?

Say that again, if you dare!

Do you remember, in 1996? That Red Cross telex from Bosnia? There was hope that time, too. A little sparkle. "Could not be identified with certainty," said the message, and it was enough to give Mom hope. Oh, not much, just a sparkle, of course, just the faintest ray, but it was enough to set the whole merry-go-round going again. Sleepless nights, buckets of coffee, and hours on the phone to God knows what aid organizations, embassies, investigation departments, slow officials, unwieldy bureaucracies, and so on. Nightly discussions, tired quarrels in the kitchen (I didn't sleep, Hugo, I heard it all), and finally Mom left for that ex-country (Croatia? Istria? Serbia?) somewhere in East Europe. Still full of hope, yes. And then, after weeks of fruitless searching and endless hoping, after days and nights in trains and planes, one day her cases were back in the hall, and Mom was on the couch, her eyes closed.

"Hey, Mom, are you all right?"

"Yes, darling, just let me be. . . ."

"Anything I can do?"

No, there was nothing I could do for her. Or, perhaps . . . (Yes? Just tell me, Mom.) Could I make her some tea? Would I like to do that? Of course Anna would like to do that. And a moment later, while Anna is busy in the kitchen, Dad storms into the house like a whirlwind, hurls himself onto the couch, and strokes Mom's graying hair. He whispers words of comfort he doesn't believe himself. Soon after, he gets up quietly and picks up the phone in the other room to ring the therapist. Could they book a follow-up session? Yes, Monday would be good, yes. And Mom is back in therapy (Monday, ten o'clock), and Dad will throw himself into his work.

And what about Anna? Anna will make tea. Anna will look after herself. Anna will cope. A bit of therapy (if that's really necessary), not too much talk, and things will be fine for Anna. Because Anna is young, she's strong.

And we're back to square one. Disbelief, anger, (hope!), protest, grief, acceptance, coming to terms, the whole rigmarole.

That was 1996, the Year of the Angry Wolf, and now it's 1999. Not again, Hugo, I've already given, *j'ai déjà donné!*

Oh, Hugo, please. Mom is all right now. Perhaps she's at her best now, better than she's ever been. Don't throw her life into confusion again with a stupid little spark of hope. False hope.

Dad? Dad is busy. Leave him alone. Dad has projects. He's busy.

And Anna? Oh, Hugo, Anna's doing fine. Anna will make

tea for Mom. Anna's a good daughter. Anna has her friends, her study, her plans. . . . Oh, Hugo, why don't you leave Anna in peace!

I screwed up the letter and chucked it into the wastepaper basket. I went to have a shower.

I turned the mixer tap from left to right and back again. Streams of hot and cold water raked my overheated body like fingers. Michael, damn you! I heard myself thinking. Why can't the bastard just stay dead! My thought frightened me.

Stop it, Anna! Stop it.

And I let the water do its work. I closed my eyes and opened my mouth. With more than usual care, I soaped myself all over, thought about Bert, and felt myself go weak. That was better. I got out of the shower, but fresh drops of sweat appeared on my forehead even while I was drying.

Then I heard the phone in the hall. My mother answered, and from her voice I could hear it was my father.

"Anna?!! Dad, for you!"

Couldn't they ever leave me alone?

How're the exams going? he would ask. Terrible, I'd reply. Come, come, he would say with a laugh. It's easy for you to laugh, I would say with a sigh. And how is your love life, he would ask next. Oh . . . so-so, I would reply.

"Anna?"

"I'm coming!"

Reluctantly I pulled a clean T-shirt over my head, yanked open the door of my room, and went downstairs.

"Hello? Yes, Dad? . . . Terrible. . . . It's easy for you to laugh. . . . What? . . . Oh . . . so-so."

I had run out of things to say, but he talked on. Fantastic weather on the coast, he said, and there was a bit of a break in his work and blah blah blah, and, as I listened to his friendly prattle, it occurred to me for the umpteenth time that it really didn't make much difference whether he was here or in Ostend. Not that I meant anything bad by that, I didn't mean anything at all, really. Just that that's how it was.

"Are you coming to see me sometime?" he asked.

He always asked that, but this time my answer gave him a bit of a shock. Me, too, for that matter.

"Day after tomorrow," I said, seeing in my mind the receiver drop out of his hand. In spite of myself, I suddenly grinned, standing there by the phone.

"Hello, Anna?"

I stifled my laugh and repeated slowly, "Day after tomorrow, Dad. I'll come and see you in Ostend the day after tomorrow. After my last exam. Is that okay?"

"Yes, of course. Yes, yes. Well, see you then, huh?"

"Okay, see you then."

As I hung up, I felt remarkably calm. And, as I had expected, Mom was suddenly standing beside me.

"What about the day after tomorrow?"

"The day after tomorrow, I'm going to see Dad. Is that okay?"

She looked at me, surprised. Anna, traveling?

"Is that okay, Mom?"

"Huh? Of course that's okay. But, are you sure . . . ?"

"I'm a big girl now, Mom."

"Mmm. . . . And?"

"And what?"

"What does he write?"

"Who?"

"Anna!"

"Oh, Hugo? I haven't read it yet."

Of course she didn't believe me. I ran to my room, slammed the door far too hard, and sat down at my desk, knees trembling. Oh, wasn't I calm! My God, I was going traveling! The day after tomorrow! Why, for God's sake, why? I walked from my desk to the window, from the window to the door, from the door to my bed, from the bed to my desk and back to the window again. I opened the curtain—sun, sun!—and watched the man from 6B letting his dog shit copiously outside 4D's garage door. Ha ha. 4D was something important in a bank or somewhere. Armani suits, dark green Mercedes. Good. A bit of shit on Mr. Important's radials would improve the world! But why did I suddenly find all of this so futile, so meaningless? So . . . ? Oh, damn it all!

I shut the curtain and fished the screwed-up letter out of my wastepaper basket. I sat behind my desk, smoothed it out, and read through it again. And then again. Then I said aloud, Okay, letter, now it's between you and me. (Oh, dear, I really did watch too much TV. This was like a cheap Western: *This town ain't big enough for the both of us!*)

All the characters in the letter (blue ballpoint, cheap

squared paper) seemed to stare at me, challenging me, but I defied it and thoughtfully tore it into strips and scattered them around me. But then it got the upper hand again, because I spent the next ten minutes busily puzzling it back together with sticky tape. It grinned, I swear I saw it grinning. Then I launched a final attack. I lit all the candles on my mantelpiece and let it tremble above the flames. That was a waste of time: it wasn't the letter that trembled, but my hand. It knew perfectly well I would blow out the licking flame at the last moment.

"Okay, letter," I muttered. "You win."

And from the depths of my wardrobe I produced my dark blue backpack and put the letter in the side pocket. Anna was about to go traveling. Tomorrow I'd pack. After the exam . . .

Shit, that exam. I grabbed my books, sat on my bed, and spent the rest of the afternoon studying history. Pretty easy, history.

Daniel Devolder

The doctor is ill

When I was four or five years old, our family doctor fell ill. Not possible, I thought. Doctors are there to cure people, not to get sick. Soon after, I fell ill myself, very ill, with such a high fever I nearly died. I was in the hospital on a drip, delirious for three days. It may sound strange, but in my childish fever dreams, images of our seriously ill Dr. Bergmans kept recurring. When I woke from my fever on the fourth day, a strange doctor stood by my bed, with my parents in the background. "Where's Dr. Bergmans?" I asked. "I'm sorry," said my father, solemn as always, and my mother threw her arms around me in tears. I was cured, but Dr. Bergmans was dead. Not possible, I thought.

Twenty years later I was a doctor myself—the second youngest doctor in Belgium—and immediately got a position as a resident. I was able to choose my own specialization and decided on tropical medicine. Full of ambition, I concentrated on research and analysis. I was going to make a huge contribution to the advance of medical science, fight strange diseases and epidemics, save mankind, no less, and in my mind I dedicated my efforts to the late Dr. Bergmans. I was a soul inspired, a full-blooded romantic in the skin of a scientist. Still am, I suppose.

Soon after, more full-blooded romance came into my life

when, through a trivial car accident, I met Frank. Filling in insurance forms together on a dented car hood—you've no idea how romantic that can be. Frank?! Love between men? Back then—I'm talking about 1966—that was still a huge taboo. But my parents—who didn't eat meat and didn't believe in God, another great taboo at that time—had told me about all sorts of love, so I recognized Frank immediately as my soul mate, and we started living together. We lived very quietly; giving offense was the last thing we wanted, and "coming out" was a concept that didn't even exist then. We lived anonymously in the big city.

A few years later we went to live even farther away. Frank belonged to some third world movement, and at his instigation I went for an African research fellowship, and we moved to Central Africa. There, I did more research into still more tropical diseases. I submitted lots of reports to the World Health Organization and became a real specialist. In 1983 we returned home. I got a good job at the Institute for Tropical Medicine in Antwerp (more science, more research), and Frank did freelance work for newspapers and magazines. Lifestyle and that sort of thing. He was good at that.

The next couple of years passed quietly. But suddenly, alarming reports started coming in from America. Some sort of gay cancer. American authorities tried to stop the news, but we were used to that. Reagan was president then, and Reagan was a cowboy, so he hated gays. At first glance, the whole thing had nothing to do with us (us? Frank and me? Belgium?

Europe?), but I rang Paris and Geneva all the same. At the Institut Pasteur in Paris they had found something, too. We know about it, they said, we're investigating it, but for the moment we can't do much. No funds, you know . . . the government . . . well, we live in hope. . . .

And for the first time my life was seriously upset. I found it impossible to grasp. And at the Pasteur Institutes in New York and Geneva it was no different: they found it impossible to grasp, too! A virus, sure, but . . . We peered into our microscopes, and we had heated telephone conversations about HIV, HIV-2, T4 cells, RNA strings, and white blood cells. I remembered a 1959 blood sample from what was then the Belgian Congo; a colleague in Geneva knew about a Norwegian sailor who had died of a mysterious disease in the late 1950s, etcetera. But the fact was that we, the tropical specialists, the absolute elite in genetics, virology, immunology, you name it, the cream of medical science—we had absolutely no idea what was happening to us. Two hundred years ago, Alfred Jenner had tamed smallpox with cows' blood, a hundred years after that, Louis Pasteur had figured out how it all worked, with antibodies and so on, and we, at the end of this twentieth century, with all our computer-aided technology, our scanners and electron microscopes, our highly advanced knowledge of DNA and RNA and enzymes and genetics, we had all been reduced to the stage of spells and enemas. What were we going to do about this?

The whole medical world was in a panic, and so was I.

Meanwhile, Frank and I were doing fine. My parents died

peacefully, posthumously wished us all happiness, and left us some money. Frank and I moved to a prosperous area on the outskirts of the city, my reputation grew, and Frank discovered new talents in himself. He started designing interiors, and did it very well.

We watched TV together in the evenings, and at times we couldn't make much sense of what was going on. I remember the summer of '85, when Live Aid boomed from all speakers and TVs on the planet: "Who's gonna take you home tonight?" Phil Collins flew from London to L.A. on the Concorde and asked us the same question on the same day on the same TV from two different continents: "Hey, boys, are you going to do anything about Africa?" Frank was furious: "You could cure a thousand leprosy sufferers for the price of one single Concorde ticket, you bastard!" We shook our heads. The world around us was becoming faster and more chaotic, and no, we couldn't keep up with it too well anymore.

Not long after, Frank fell ill. It started with a persistent cough, and after a few examinations it was clear: he had "it." For the second time in my life I began to doubt everything I had taken for granted, and to think seriously about chance and fate, about science and certainty. About transience and humility, that sort of thing. I kept on peering into those microscopes, and meanwhile Frank needed oxygen. The end came barely two years later, in a bed in the University Hospital at Wilrijk. I stood by his white bed and held his wrist in my hand. Doctor. His arm was no more than a bone.

And he was only forty! "Life begins at forty," said John Lennon, and *bang!* went Mark Chapman. Exit Lennon: 12/8/1980, 11:00 P.M.

Frank died on 3/6/1988. He didn't want to be buried. His ashes blew on the wind in a garden of rest somewhere south of Antwerp. I thought of the sea. Colleagues told me, "Have some rest, Devolder. Go on a trip." But I hung my stethoscope round my neck and went back to wandering through the wards of the University Hospital. My head was filled with memories of Frank, and I thought about my dream of science as a passion, saving humanity. Words like *mortal* and *powerless* didn't fit in that dream. To tell the truth, I was desperate.

The wards filled. The patients were young, much younger even than Frank. I stood by their beds, day and night, and talked to them. I examined them, prescribed drugs, new cocktails, AZT (miracle drug! ah!), but I couldn't help them. They were young, the poor bastards, so young, but sometimes they knew more about life than all of us, their doctors, put together. One of them gave me a gift: of a book of photos. With trembling hand he inscribed a dedication. I leafed through the book. "Nothing but people, Doc," he said, sucking air through his plastic oxygen mask. "Some of them are dead already, some of them are still alive, but you'll never know who's alive and who's not. Weird things, photos, aren't they?" Two days later he was dead.

And again I felt powerless.

Then I fell ill myself.

One day, I suddenly felt dizzy in one of those white hospital corridors, and everything started spinning around me. I remember tearing my stethoscope from my neck, as if it were suffocating me. Hours later, I woke up in a white bed. A colleague was holding my wrist. "It's your heart," he said. I had to laugh. Of course it was my heart. "Broken, I suppose?" I said foolishly, but he raised his eyebrows high, muttering something about heart chambers and narrowed aortas. Very amusing. Our profession has never been guilty of excessive humor, but I must admit, what he said really wasn't anything to laugh about. I'd never be able to work again, he said. If I took it easy, I might have five, at most ten years ahead of me. If.

Ahead of me, like some task. For some reason, I thought of the sea again. I loved the sea. I always spent holidays with Frank by the sea. . . . And suddenly, my mind was made up. The circle was closed. I was now a sick doctor.

As soon as I was discharged from the hospital, I called an estate agent and the movers. Ostend it would be.

The sea.

Nothing else.

(And Frank's photo, in my inside pocket.)

Anna

Train trip to the seaside, part one

Two days later (after a satisfactory history exam, thank you) I stood on platform 1 of Louvain Station at 7:33 A.M. And I wondered what in God's name I was doing there.

I hated traveling.

In my imagination, planes always fell out of the sky, trains were invariably delayed for hours, cars were unavoidably caught in monstrous traffic jams, and touring buses always crashed into ravines. Always. The mere scent of sunblock was enough to make me feel nauseous, school trips were nightmares that I mostly spent in the bus being sick, and all I remembered of the annual holidays with my parents was the joy of coming home.

I have never been more grateful to my mother than two years ago, when she finally and at long last let me off. While she, in the company of my father and a couple million other idiots, journeyed down a steaming hot motorway to southern lands "to get away from it all," I was allowed to stay home by myself.

Stay home by myself! Heaven on earth. Never had I enjoyed a holiday so much: fry an egg, watch MTV till two o'clock in the morning, eat an apple, read a book in the garden, wander around our deserted streets. . . . (The last Easter break had been especially good, because Bert had stayed home, too, and we'd given the words *Home Alone* a whole new meaning. But that's another story.)

Dr. Dirk, who used to be my therapist, suggested during one of our infrequent sessions that my travel phobia had something to do with my two big brothers, Jonas and Michael, who were away so often that on the odd occasion they came home they needed to reserve their rooms, like in a hotel.

"Yes, great, but not really, Dr. Dirk. I've had this travel phobia much longer than that, since I was six or seven, when I wasn't yet bothered by faraway dead brothers."

Dr. Dirk opened a folder.

"Well, Anna . . . when Jonas left for America you were six, or have I got that wrong?"

"Yes, but," I said, "I didn't mind then. I thought it was exciting, having a big brother in America."

"And at about that time your other brother Michael left for Italy. . . ."

"Yes, but I didn't mind then. That's what I said."

"You really didn't?"

"No."

I looked around me. The platform was deserted apart from two or three people, but they were staring so vacantly, they hardly counted as living beings. In actual fact I was alone on that platform, totally alone, thinking about a holiday by the sea that happened nearly ten years ago.

I was seven or eight; Jonas was already in America and Michael in Italy, but my father thought we should all go to the beach together. All together, that was Mom, him, and me. Ha ha. On the day we were to leave, I hid in the cupboard under the sink. My mother ran around all the rooms; my father sat behind the wheel, blowing the horn. It took nearly an hour before they found me, and by that time my father was so furious he dragged me into the car by my hair. In revenge I didn't say a word to him for three days (lovely holiday, there by the sea), and on the fourth day, in a fit of fury, he took me to Ostend station. "Okay, have it your way! Go home by yourself! Here's your ticket!" And there I stood, clutching one of those cardboard tickets, in the middle of hundreds of fat, sweating bodies, wrapped in the most hideous clothes, wearing black sunglasses, speaking incomprehensible languages. Soon after, a monstrous great train rolled hissing into the station (it made me think of a dragon), and those hundreds of puffing tourists hoisted themselves into it, all those suitcases and shorts and fat bodies, and I stood there paralyzed. The train pulled out, and then, suddenly, that platform was so empty, so empty. . . . Less than a minute later, my father came to get me, of course, but to me it felt as if I had stood there for hours. "Hey, Anna," he said with a shy smile, getting ready to hug me, but I pressed the crumpled-up ticket into his hand.

"Really, Anna? You really didn't mind then?"

"No, Dr. Dirk, I really didn't. . . ."

Meanwhile, it was 7:53, and dead on time (strange!), the train rolled into the station.

It was one of those sad-looking dark green trains that only seem fit to transport masses of yawning commuters to the capital, but it was Saturday, so there were no commuters. The doors swung open with a hiss, and I stepped into the train as inconspicuously as I could, thinking of a Nick Cave song: "Today she took a train to the west."

Without commuters, the train looked even more sad and pointless, and I was almost surprised when it ground into action again and dutifully started moving in the direction of the coast. Just for me? It seemed rather like that. I looked around, almost in a panic. Where was I going again? And what was I going there for?

But then I thought of the letter in the side pocket of my backpack, and realized I had no choice. Or rather, that I'd already made the choice. And another choice confronted me immediately: one hundred and eighty empty seats, and which one would be mine?

After a long hesitation, I chose a spacious window seat, facing forward, about halfway down the carriage. I hoisted my far-too-heavy backpack into the luggage rack, put my camera bag on the seat next to me, and sat down. Then I changed my mind, stood up again, took my backpack from the luggage rack, unzipped the side pocket, and felt for my book and my ticket. My fingers registered the letter next to my ticket. No, not right now, letter! I took the ticket and the book, zipped up my backpack, hoisted it back onto the rack, and flopped down on the seat. I put the book next to me on top of the camera bag, put the somewhat crushed ticket on the foldout table in front of me, and smoothed it with my hand for the benefit of the conductor.

I had just finished when the connecting door of the carriage slid open. The conductor, I thought, but it wasn't.

It was a tall, thin man, graying at the temples, wearing a cream-colored three-piece suit. His eyes looked clear and mild, and his eyebrows were raised high, as if in a constant state of surprise. But most striking were his hat and his nose, both unusually large. Perhaps he had to wear the one to hide the other.

Slowly looking around, he walked down the carriage, and I could feel it coming. Oh no, I thought, not again, please, no, not again, not like in the cinema. But yes, of course, it was just like in the cinema. My fate, always. One hundred and seventy-nine free seats, and he sat immediately opposite me. And he was well over six feet tall.

He smiled at me amiably and sat down with a flowing movement, crossing his legs fastidiously—almost as if he folded himself up—taking care to avoid mine. His socks matched his tie exactly, I noticed at a glance: bright red. He took off his hat, put it on his lap, and unfolded a newspaper. Phew.

A center-left-green coalition was about to form a government, I read, and the extreme right loudly disagreed with this (surprise, surprise); the dioxin crisis was costing the agricultural sector something like four or five million a day, and the last solar eclipse of this century was going to take place on August 11. I also learned that huge traffic jams were being caused in Kosovo by fleeing Serbs and returning Albanians, and that we (we? who, we?) had beaten Switzerland 3–1. The world was coming at me through thick black type, but what did I have to do with the world?

I decided to concentrate on the window. Better the world behind glass than the printed world. I used my hands like a pair of binoculars, letting a series of images pass in front of my eyes: parched meadows, wheezing cows drinking from rusty old bathtubs, industrial areas, shopping centers, cell phone towers, greenhouses, fallow fields, new housing estates full of identical villas with identical cypress trees and identical front gardens, clotheslines full of underwear, and bridges full of graffiti (*NATO kills*). It made me a bit dizzy. So this was traveling. I thought of the letter in my backpack.

The train stopped three times in Brussels. In a bit of a daze, I watched people moving about on the platforms. They'd all come from somewhere, or had to go somewhere. I couldn't understand what drove them all. A couple of times I looked at the man opposite me, hoping vaguely each time he would get off, but he didn't stir. Shit. Almost soundlessly we left the capital behind.

The landscape behind the glass turned green and bare again, and I began to feel a bit more peaceful. I shut my eyes and tried to think. Letter, Michael, Hugo, Mom. Dad, Ostend, train, Rovinj. Bert, Hugo, Kristel, "Believe," ticket, letter. It was a bit chaotic in my head.

Then, somewhere between Brussels and Ghent, I suddenly heard a voice.

"Excuse me, please."

I nearly died of fright. The man in the red socks had folded up his newspaper and was now leaning over toward me, his nose aimed straight at me like some kind of weapon, and his bulbous eyes staring at me questioningly from behind his glasses. Oh, my God. I started back, and his lips moved.

"I'm terribly sorry if I frightened you," the lips spoke, "but I was intrigued by your camera bag."

He spoke the way he was dressed. Old-fashioned, but with a curious accent.

I was silent. As long as I remained silent, he would automatically shut up, I thought. But he didn't.

"I see that you distrust me, and I can't blame you," he said with a smile. "Especially these days."

These days? Oh yes, of course. Shit, what a thing to say. If I kept quiet now, it would show I distrusted him (feeble and predictable), which I didn't want. But of course I did distrust him. Especially these days, as he had said. Shit.

I looked at him as coldly as I could, but my look didn't have the desired effect. He smiled and continued.

"Possibility one: I am a dirty old man who is after your sweet young body. Why else would I have sat straight opposite you in an empty carriage?"

So why don't you move, you bastard? I thought furiously. But my thoughts didn't have the desired effect either. He stayed where he was.

"Possibility two is even worse: I really am the big bad wolf with the white van, and I have a bottle of chloroform in my pocket."

Talk about sick! If this was meant to be joke, it was a particularly nauseating one. My look was apparently getting more eloquent, as he went on quickly.

"Possibility three: I am gay, and you have no reason to distrust me because you're female."

What? Now he had really surprised me, and I let myself be caught.

"Is that so?" I blabbed, but he wasn't fazed. Or he was deaf.

"Possibility four," he said. "I am genuinely interested in your camera bag, because I really like photography."

This last bit sounded so genuinely friendly that I had to smile despite myself. After that, being silent wasn't really an option. But I didn't quite give in, yet. At least a small counter-attack first. I leaned back, looking at him through my lashes.

"Possibility five—" I said.

"Well?"

"You're just an intrusive bore who bothers young, defenseless victims in nearly empty railway carriages with the story of his life because he's afraid of his own loneliness."

Wow. That hit the mark. I was shocked myself. So was he.

"Touché," he said with an appreciative smile.

"I prefer looking out the window," I said as rudely as I could.

"You're perfectly entitled to. Well, then, if you prefer to be silent and look out, just say so. I'm still happy to talk."

I began to relax.

"Can I think about that for a minute?" I asked.

Now he laughed out loud. His teeth had brown edges. A smoker's teeth.

"Go right ahead," he said.

Despite myself, I began to find this conversation amusing, and despite my fears and despite his nose, the man wasn't really repulsive. I weighed the alternatives.

It was at least another hour to the coast, the view from the window was pretty monotonous, and my mind was in no fit state for reading. That left two possibilities: a mental struggle with the chaos in my head, or a conversation with an aging gay photographer.

I made up my mind. For a moment I kept pretending, looking up at the plastic roof of the carriage, rolling my eyes, and then I said, "Okay."

"Okay what?"

"Talk."

"Sure?"

"Yes."

"Good." He shifted in his seat. "What'll we talk about?"

"Which of the five possibilities are actually true?" I asked.

"Three, four, and five," he said, without batting an eyelid.

"So you really are gay and interested in my camera bag?"

He nodded with a smile. I unzipped the bag for him.

"Here you are. Have a look."

"No need."

"No?"

"Only a tourist would put a Minolta in a Nikon bag."

Aha, an expert. Was he a photographer?

"At best a creditable amateur," he replied. "But I would love to know why you take photos."

"And I would love to know who you are."

"Of course. Excuse me. Unforgivable—" and he held out his hand. "Daniel Devolder."

"Anna," I nodded, and after a brief hesitation I shook his hand.

"Anna," he muttered. "Nice name."

"You think so? I don't."

"It's reversible. I like reversible names."

"Really? So you'd have liked to be called Otto or something?"

He laughed again, exposing his brown teeth, and I pulled my hand back.

"So, are you going to tell me?"

"What?"

"Why you take photos?"

I shrugged. "Just because. It's fun. Click, and a piece of the world is in the box. Simple, really—"

"People? Landscapes?"

"Never people," I replied truthfully. I'd never wanted a person in front of my lens. And certainly not anyone in my family. Not my mother, not my father, not my friends. I hadn't even taken Bert's photo. I didn't dare.

"Never?"

I shook my head.

"Why?"

"People are too . . . complicated. To photograph, I mean."

"I like people. I like looking at them."

"So do I, but—" From a distance, I wanted to say, but checked myself.

Fortunately, he changed the subject.

"Color or black-and-white?" he asked.

"Black-and-white," I replied, relieved. "I don't like color. Color is too busy. Too much all at once."

"Color is more realistic. Closer to reality."

"Color is noisy. Black-and-white is"—I had to search for the right word—"clearer. More precise. Quieter. Deeper."

He nodded thoughtfully. "Black-and-white photos also tend to look rather antique, don't you think? Like something from the past."

His tone had become more familiar, I noticed, but it didn't bother me. What did bother me was that I was suddenly thinking about the past again. In a flash, a black-and-white photo appeared before my eyes, sharply focused. A photo from the past. I could feel myself getting tense. Perhaps this conversation wasn't such a good idea after all, Anna. But fortunately he was already steering the conversation in a different direction, whether he meant to or not.

"Do you do your own printing?"

"Of course. I've got a darkroom set up in the bathroom."

And so on, and so on, and gradually I relaxed. For the next half hour we held what's called "a pleasant conversation." He told me things about photography I already knew, and some I didn't, and he listened to me, as if he found my remarks interesting. It became the sort of conversation you can keep going effortlessly without revealing anything personal, and that suited me. The world slid past us and time flew, and by the time we were moving through Ghent, I was so relaxed that I had the bright idea of telling this Devolder I might study photography in the year of grace 1999–2000. It would have been better if I hadn't.

"Photography," he said. "Yes, of course, yes. But, Anna, then you must never forget one thing!" And he pointed with his long index finger.

"And what's that?"

"The strength of a photo lies in what is absent."

"What is absent?"

Ghent was well behind us now, and for the first time in a long while I looked out the window. The landscape behind the glass was flat. Scrawny trees bending with the wind, hazy pastureland and dried-out ditches. Small farmhouses with broken-backed roofs, and churches like lighthouses glimpsed between industrial estates. We were rapidly approaching the coast, and my travel phobia changed into another sort of fear. My fear of the past. This was my father's flat country, the land where he was born, where his roots were, where he had met Mom; where he used to drag us for holiday after holiday, and where he himself had now, finally, taken refuge. I tried to imagine what my meeting with him would be like, but couldn't. The flat country, the sea: it was getting close. My father. Hugo. I was getting nervous again.

Devolder hadn't noticed anything.

"Look," he said. "A photo is an image. And an image, by definition, stands for something else. For a reality. A reality we must be without. And the image replaces that reality, at least temporarily. So a photo helps people to relive, in a very limited way, a reality they are forced to be without. To fill an absence, in other words. Do you understand?"

"Er . . . sort of."

"You don't, then. I'll give you an example: people in love. What do they do? They give each other a photo of themselves and put it in their inside pocket."

"You're in my pocket, my love . . . right over my heart." Oh, yes!

"Exactly!" he said. "The photo in the inside pocket—"

"—is a flat and reduced version of your sweetheart."

"Quite so. But you only need it when—"

"Er . . . when, when . . . er . . . I don't know."

"When your love isn't there. For when your love is there—"

"—then you look at the real thing, not at a stupid photo."

"*Voilà*," he said. I felt like a very good student. "Good," he went on. "But suppose you split up. Then what do you do?"

Alarm! I bristled. If there was one situation I was familiar with, this was it. Sixteen times in three years, to be exact. No, seventeen. Forgot Bert for a moment. Oh, Bert. But I wasn't about to let Mr. Daniel Devolder in on my inner secrets, no matter how charming I found him. So I shrugged with a bit of a giggle.

"I kill him."

"Carries a life sentence. Or a minimum ten years with mitigating circumstances. Come on, Anna, you know perfectly well what I mean. You don't kill him, but you do kill . . ."

I felt myself going pale. This wasn't going the right way, not at all. This conversation really hadn't been such a good idea. Oh, no, please, I thought, don't let him say it, please, no. But he said it anyway.

"You kill the photo, of course! Your ex-love isn't there, so you attack something you do have handy: the image. Isn't that strange? All your hatred, your fury, your grief, are concentrated on that stupid, harmless two-by-three-inch piece of paper, and while you rip it up, with all the bottled-up and now useless passion that is still in your body, you have the feeling you are attacking the person himself. Attacking the person himself, truly, with real murderous intent! The proof? Just think of the relief you feel when you see the shreds blowing away on the wind or burning in the fireplace, that strange sense of relief that instantly gets mixed up with thoughts of crime: You should be locked up for doing this. My God, what sort of sentence would you get for that, for ripping up a photo? But it's not so surprising you feel like that, for you really have destroyed someone, a person."

I had become very quiet. And he noticed.

"Is something wrong?" he asked.

I tried to smile. "No, not at all. It's nothing."

But then, suddenly, there really was something wrong. He raised his finger, as if he was about to say something else important, but he didn't say it. Instead he turned deathly pale, his face twisted with pain, the long fingers of his right hand clawed at his chest, and his forehead was instantly covered in thick beads of sweat. I could see them break out, those drops, one by one. It was as if they were crowding on the inside of his skull for the start of a race, and they kept streaming out—*gushing* would have been the right word, I think. Incredible how much sweat could gush through those pores in a few seconds—it was like the river Meuse in full flood.

With one hand he grabbed for his red tie, tried to loosen it, tugging and jerking it, while his other hand reached for his vest pocket in a kind of cramp. He managed to extract a small, gold-colored pillbox from it—just like him to carry such a neat little thing, I thought in a flash—clicked it open with trembling fingers, and shook a couple of pills into his mouth. One missed his gaping lips and fell down his collar, and another one rolled down his coat to the floor. Involuntarily, I followed it with my eyes until it came to rest under a seat across the aisle. Just like when you hit a wild ball at tennis and remember exactly where it disappears into the shrubs outside the wire netting (for later, when you're going to pick it up, after the game), so the exact spot where that pill rolled was engraved on my mind. For later.

Meanwhile, Devolder was leaning back with his eyes closed, breathing in and out deeply, his hand moving back and forth over his chest. I could see he was in pain. His face was somewhere between ash gray and yellow, and he continued to sweat heavily.

"Excuse me," he muttered, panting. "It happens to me more and more often, lately. I'll really have to watch it."

His voice roused me, and I realized that I hadn't moved through the whole episode. As if I had been watching a film. If I could, I might have zapped the whole business away. Oh, Anna, what now? Just for something to do, I went and picked up the pill that had rolled away and put it on the table in front of him. Like a lost tennis ball. But his eyes were still closed, so I didn't get much of a reaction. Should I say something?

"Er . . . Are you all right?"

He nodded weakly. Was there anything I should be doing (other than picking up his pill)?

"Er . . . Is there anything I can do? Call the conductor, pull the emergency brake? Get something to drink?"

Leave it, he waved me away. Yet I said something else, something completely absurd, but I said it anyway.

"Shall I get a doctor?"

He laughed briefly. "I'm a doctor myself, Anna."

A doctor? I could see him as all sorts of things, but not as a doctor. Now I really didn't know what to say, but I felt I ought to keep talking. That's what they do with someone who has swallowed too many sleeping pills—I'd seen it on TV.

"Er . . . Is it your heart?"

"The heart is just a muscle, you know."

I always get scared when people talk to me with their eyes closed.

"Yes, I know, but—"

"Don't worry, it's all over. It's still beating."

"What?"

"My heart. It's still beating."

"Oh." Tongue-tied again. Say something, Anna, for God's sake!

But suddenly his eyes were wide open, clear, and looking straight at me. I got a fright. This had happened to me before. Very lively eyes, just before they closed for good. What was going on with this Devolder?

"Anna?"

"Yes?"

"Don't get a fright. In just a moment I'm going to—"

"What? What?"

He put a finger to his lips. "In just a moment I'm going to fall asleep. But I'm not going to die. So you mustn't be frightened."

"But?"

"Ssh." He put a finger to his lips once more and leaned back. His eyes closed again. Like the curtain after the performance.

"I'm tired," he muttered. "Just leave me be, okay?"

He slumped in his seat a bit: sank down into it, I thought. Sink, sank, sunk. I clapped my hand over my mouth; he wouldn't be able to see that, anyway. Oh, no. He wouldn't be . . . ? Don't be scared, Anna. But the next moment I could see he was breathing gently. He was asleep.

Strange. I relaxed, allowing myself to sink down into the

seat, too. It was like watching a sleeping child. As if I was baby-sitting for someone. And I was pleased he seemed to trust me.

He was still fast asleep when the conductor came into the carriage a little later. Carefully I pulled his ticket out of his inside pocket, where I had noticed it when he was getting his pillbox out, smiled at the conductor, and put a finger over my lips.

"Your father seems to be very tired." The man nodded while he clipped the tickets.

"He works too hard," I said, like a concerned daughter.

He touched his clipper to his cap and went on his way. I looked at the tickets. Mine was creased all over, his smooth as the tabletop, and I thought of the battered letter in the side pocket of my backpack, and I thought of a photo I had ripped up years ago.

On July 24, 1994, to be exact. The day I had my last fit of fury. Well, the second-to-last one.

Irina

Normally, I wouldn't dream of doing this

I stood by the front door, looking for my key, when the phone rang. Pierre, I thought. I found the key just in time, dashed into the hall, and picked up the phone. I was quite out of breath.

"Hello. Irina here."

"Mrs. Bracke?"

"Yes, but . . ."

It wasn't Pierre, it was Bert.

Bert? Bert? Oh, of course, *that* Bert.

"Anna isn't here, Bert. I've just driven her to the station."

"Oh. Can I catch her there?"

No, he couldn't. She was off to the beach, to see her father, and he had an unlisted number. And yes, I appreciated that he had to speak to her urgently, but I really couldn't help him. Sorry.

"Okay, I'll find her myself, then," he said.

"Do what you think best," I said and hung up.

A bit curt? Probably. But really, Anna and her friends, I wasn't going to get involved. And anyway, I had more important things to do.

I checked my watch: seven-thirty. Plenty of time. I went up the stairs, and even though I was quite alone in the house, I avoided the fourth tread because it had a squeak. Just as if

I was seventeen again, coming home late from a party. You're doing really well, Irina!

In front of the door of her room I looked nervously over my shoulder, bit my lip, and turned the doorknob. Not locked. Anna trusted me. That only made it worse.

But I went in all the same. Her bed was made, as if she would be gone for a long time. Almost nothing on the walls. Several lighter patches in the wallpaper where she'd removed all her posters a year ago. No more pop groups. I had wanted to paint over it, but hadn't gotten around to it. There were just two photographs. Black-and-white. A sunset, somewhere in America. Ansel Adams, I read. And one showing two dancers in Harlem, New York.

New York.

Her wardrobe stood open. Before closing it, I had a quick look at the empty hangers. She had taken far too much for two days. I hadn't said anything, because I knew how much she hated that. Oh, my little girl!

She had been so brave just then, at the station. She kissed me on the cheek and picked up her heavy backpack and her camera bag. "Shall I give you a hand carrying that?" I asked.

"No need. See you the day after tomorrow, Mom."

"Bye, darling."

My eyes followed her while she made her way through the chaos of the station forecourt, through the hoardings, the trench diggers, and the excavations, and I felt a lump in my throat. Anna was traveling. The sea is a long way off, and two days is a long time, for Anna.

I sat down behind her desk. Her history book was there, her last subject. She'd written "*Fini*. For Good" in thick felt pen on its cover. Blushing with shame, I pushed the book aside, took a deep breath, and did something I had never, but absolutely never done before.

I searched her room.

In the bottom drawer of her desk I found drafts of farewell letters to Kurt, and Bram, and David (she was pretty careless with those drafts, I'd found one among the phone bills, once). In another drawer I found a fair number of Mars Bar and Snickers wrappers (no surprise there, I knew she secretly snacked while studying), and in another a packet of condoms. Well, what did I expect? I had often insisted she must always make sure she had . . . You know, with boys . . . "Yes, Mom, I know!"

I swallowed and searched on.

In the wastepaper basket I found a couple of half-burned scraps of letter paper, and some torn-off bits of sticky tape. I was shocked. Was this it? Had she burned it? Didn't she want anything to do with it anymore? But what about the sticky tape? Perhaps she'd wanted to burn it, but had had second thoughts . . .

God, how terrible! Oh, I didn't want this, I didn't want this! I slapped my hand over my mouth, bit my fist. And suddenly I found myself sobbing in my daughter's desk chair. I felt mean and nasty.

But why hadn't she told me anything? Anything at all about that letter! I had hoped that when I took her to the station she might . . . just something, a word, even just a hint. Oh God, what hadn't I hoped for?

But nothing. Nothing, nothing, nothing. Not a word.

Hugo, damn it. What had he written?

In my mind I grabbed Anna by the shoulders and shook her. Tell me! I have a right to know. It's my son, you know, I have a right! Because of course that letter was about Michael! What else would it be about? Who else? A letter from Rovinj, Croatia! Why else would Hugo write? Tell me, Anna, speak, please, say something! I know, it's your letter, it's addressed to you, but please, say something. *Speak to me!*

In a rage, I pulled open every drawer of her desk, jumped up, pulled everything out of her wardrobe, even searched under the mattress.

I leaned against the doorjamb in despair. I should have known. She'd taken it with her. If it was of any importance at all, she would've taken that letter with her. Torn up, half-burned, stuck together again with sticky tape.

Oh, Irina, what are you doing? Forgive me, Anna, I'm sorry, darling. You've had to be silent so much, these last few years. Sorry, sorry. And there has been so much silence around you. But I thought all was well between us now. Anna? Anna?

I slunk out of the room like a thief, pulling the door shut very quietly. I picked up the phone and dialed her father's number. Answering machine. I hung up. No, no message. Call back later. Hugo, then? I still knew his number by heart. Another answering machine.

Who else? Who else could I call? Oh, God.

Anna

War of the Roses—train trip to the seaside, part two

On July 24, 1994, my parents came to pick me up. They had been away for more than three months, and all that time I had been staying with Uncle Paul and Aunt Lydia in Diest. It had been a strange period, to put it mildly. A few weeks after Jonas's death, Mama went off traveling, first to Italy, to stay with Michael, then to America and Jonas's friends there. Dad was "very busy." Work, they told me in Diest, but I understood, of course, that it all had to do with Jonas. At that time, my parents were both very preoccupied with their grief for Jonas. On my birthday (June 12) they came to collect me in Diest. They had even brought me a present (a Barbie doll, can you believe it? I was *eleven!*), but after only a few days they had to be off, to Italy again, together this time. "Only a few days, Anna."

"But *why?*" I asked. But they wouldn't say. I had to go back to Diest. They were being terribly mysterious about this last trip, but I knew perfectly well what they were going to do there, because Aunt Lydia had told my cousin Stef. They were going to scatter Jonas's ashes, on a hill somewhere in Italy. Children often understand more than parents.

Anyway, on that twenty-fourth of July they finally came to get me. I was really going home. Exuberant and affectionate greetings, not a cloud in the sky. I was so pleased to see them again, they were so pleased to see me again, Uncle Paul and Aunt Lydia were so pleased to get rid of me (joke!), elaborate kissing and hugging all round, and "bye-bye" and "thanks" and "look after yourself." But during the drive back to Holsbeek, all the loss and loneliness of the past months suddenly came to the surface. Three times I made them stop the car, pretending I was sick. And the moment the front door of our house slammed shut behind us, I exploded. I screamed, stamped my feet, cried, threw chairs, smashed things. It was like *The War of the Roses* (awful film!). And then, while my parents just stood there, like beaten dogs, their suitcases still in their hands, tanned from the Italian sun—that's when I tore up the photo.

It wasn't standing on the mantelpiece, it wasn't even framed, it just hung next to the kitchen door, stuck to the wall with four drawing pins. Sixteen by twenty inches, black-and-white. Michael and Jonas in the garden.

Death, I thought. I don't want it. This is a photo of death. Don't want anything to do with it.

And I ripped it off the wall, that stupid sheet of photo paper, and holding it in front of me with my arms stretched out, between thumbs and forefingers, defiantly, tauntingly, right under my parents' eyes—eyes full of dismay and confusion—before those eyes, with ritual precision, I slowly tore the photo into two pieces. Tore Michael away from Jonas. Separated death and life. Briefly.

Yes, certainly, Mr. Devolder. Illusion, absence, magic—it was all of those. He was still sleeping, his head leaning against the window, his glasses slipped down his nose. I gently took them off and put them on the foldout table.

After my fit of fury, I ran to my room crying, and was totally silent for three weeks. Powerful weapon, that kind of silence. Jonas was good at it too, according to Dad. And Dad too, according to Mama. And me too, of course, according to everybody. And my parents, most of all, according to me. Anyway, sometime during those weeks my parents decided we couldn't go on like that, because the following Monday I had my first appointment with Dr. Dirk.

"Why are you so angry, Anna?"

Shrug. None of his bloody business, that pain in the neck with his scholarly-looking glasses.

"Who are you angry with, Anna?"

None of your business, buddy.

"Listen, Anna, I would like us to come to an agreement, you and I . . ."

An agreement with you, bug-eyes? I'd sooner drop dead.

"Here, inside this room"—gesturing broadly, proud as a peacock of his super-trendy office with leather couches and Levolor blinds and framed certificates on the wall—"in this room you can say anything you like. Anything at all. Nobody, except the two of us, will ever know."

Says you, slimeball!

"If you want to be angry, just be angry—but be a bit careful with that painting there, I'm rather attached to it."

Oh ho, a joke! Ha, ha!

"If you want to cry, cry as hard as you like. If you want to be silent, just be silent."

"I'll be silent then," I said abruptly.

So ended my first session with Doctor Dirk, and began a year of being silent.

At about that point I must have fallen asleep, too. It sounds strange, but it's true. If I have to think of too many things at once, or if the emotions become too heavy, I fall asleep. Dr. Dirk said once that it is, *was*, a kind of defense mechanism. Suppose it is. And that's how, on that lovely June morning, in that depressing dark green train on its way to the coast, in the company of a middle-aged stranger with a heart condition who was fast asleep, I fell asleep, too. A fine pair we made.

When I woke up, we were close to the sea. I could smell it. It smelled of rotten eggs and smoldering plastic. My father had told me about the stink from the large chemical factory in Zandburg, a few miles from Ostend. When the wind blew the wrong way, the whole town stank.

Still half asleep, I looked through the window. The landscape around the factory was even flatter than the rest of the countryside. Beaten flat. It was as if that factory couldn't bear anything anywhere near it, not a tree, not a cow, not a hedge, not a house. Not even another factory. Only flat wasteland, bare and dry. The factory itself looked like a cross between Auschwitz and a postmodern cultural center, a complicated construction of colorful steel pipes with an enormous concrete-and-barbed-wire fence around it, and it was the size of a small town.

Had Devolder smelled it, too? A few moments after me, he woke up from his deep sleep, stretched, and turned to me again. I was glad to see him like that, alive and well. He cleared his throat and said, as if nothing had happened, "Mm, nearly there."

"Aha, you're alive?"

"And hope to keep it that way for a while yet." He pointed outside. "We're nearly home."

"Do you live here, then?"

"From now on, yes. And you?"

"My father lives here. Anyway . . . I'm only staying a few days." Again, I felt slightly uneasy under his glance. He looked at me searchingly, as if I reminded him of someone. I asked, "Are you really a doctor?"

"Was," he said, brushing an imaginary bit of dust from his sleeve. "I *was* a doctor."

"And now?" I insisted.

"We're there," he said.

The train slowed down. I watched him sideways while he got up. With an immaculate white handkerchief, he wiped some fresh sweat from his forehead before putting on his equally immaculate white hat. He looked good. Particularly for someone . . .

"For someone my age with a heart problem, I don't look too bad, don't you think?"

I flushed.

He laughed, reached in his inside pocket, and handed me a card. "It's still full of boxes," he said apologetically. "I've just moved. But do drop in if you feel like it."

"Why?"

"I've got a great view of the sea."

"My father has that, too."

"I thought as much. But anyway, here's my card."

The train had been stationary for a while, he had got out and disappeared among the crowd on the platform, but I still stood staring at that card. His old address had been crossed out with a ballpoint pen, and the new one written above it in a neat, old-fashioned hand. The address was the same apartment block as my father's.

Pierre

The sea is so clear

I'm beginning to realize that I've always lived by the sea, really. Even when I wasn't actually living there anymore. And I realize it even more now that I'm back here.

That sounds pretty confused, and so it is. In my head, I mean.

And yet, if someone were to ask me what the sea means to me, I'd answer, Clarity. Lucidity. Knowing where you stand. A worldview. Balance. That sort of thing.

I was born here, you see.

Still sounds confused, I know.

Shall I tell you about the tram? The tram along the beach? Maybe that'll clarify things in my head, too.

I was born in a smallish village by the sea, and when I was eleven, I had to go to the big school in the big city. Sixth grade. The big city, that was Ostend. Every day, five miles there and five miles back. On the coastal tram. And most of the route ran along the beach. In the morning, the sea was on our left, in the evening to our right. And that's where it came from, that sense of clarity.

That lucidity.

On that tram. For seven years, every school day: on the left in the morning, on the right in the evening, but it was always there, the sea.

Once, I saw a seagull on my right, and I kept watching that gull. Five miles it flew along with the tram, above the sea, without beating its wings a single time. And that tram was doing easily forty or fifty.

And all at once I understood what the sea meant for me. For us, children of the coast. The sea drew a clear line through our world. Children who didn't live by the sea had a three-hundred-and-sixty-degree view. We had one of a hundred and eighty. For us, children of the coast, half of our world would always be open. Open, inaccessible, awe-inspiring, slightly threatening, endless, flat.

Years later, when I went to study architecture (in an inland city, far from the sea), I came to understand something else: The sea could never be built over. That sort of understanding is important, you know. You simply don't know these days where they're going to build next. The house you have saved so hard for looks out over peaceful grassland with the occasional cow. "What a lovely view you've got here," visiting friends exclaim. But suddenly some guys in a local government office somewhere get busy with colored pencils and erasers, a regional plan is amended, the grassland is rezoned, and before you know where you are, you've got earth-moving machinery in your backyard and a six-story apartment building by your backdoor. Farewell lovely view! These days, no one can be certain of their horizon.

Except by the sea. The sea you can count on. They'll never build over the sea. The mere idea!

That's why I get so angry when some idiot developer

turns up with a "project" to fill up a bit of the sea with concrete to build a causeway or an artificial island or something!

You don't build over the sea! You keep your dirty hands off the sea! Full stop!

So that's the sort of thing I was thinking about, standing by the open window of my new home by the sea (Temporary? Permanent? Temporarily permanent? Hmm), looking out over the open, inaccessible, slightly threatening, awe-inspiring and ever-flat one hundred and eighty degrees of my world. I lit a cigar (only the first one that morning, and it was already nearly nine), when the phone rang. It was Irina.

"Pierre?" she said.

"Who else?" I said.

She sighed. "Anna is on her way."

"I know," I said. "She called me."

"I know," she said. (Oh, communication!)

"So why are you calling?" I asked. (Oh, logic!)

"No particular reason," she said. "Just to make sure . . ."

"Make sure of what?" I asked.

"That you're there," she said.

"Oho," I said. "That again? That I'm never there? Was never there? Is that what we're talking about again?"

"Pierre!" She sounded tired. I guessed she was already at work.

"Yes, okay. Sorry. Tell me."

"I think Anna is not her usual self—"

"I noticed that, too."

"Oh, yes?"

"Yes, I had noticed that, too!" I said rather loudly. (Pierre never notices anything.)

"I'm sorry!" she said, even louder.

(Irina and I always say "sorry" and "please" a lot when we're quarreling. People who are quarreling are often much more polite than people who aren't.)

Then I said, a bit more softly, "What makes you think so?" I could hear her swallow.

"Listen, Pierre," she said. "Anna has been strange lately. She has broken off with her boyfriend again—"

"That's not so strange."

"I know. But then she suddenly wanted to travel, to go to see you—"

"That I did find strange, yes. That's what made me take notice. Particularly with her travel phobia."

"Exactly." And she said it as if it was the most normal thing in the world. "I'm going to see Dad."

"Exactly. That's how it sounded to me, too. . . . Irina?"

"Yes?"

"Has anything in particular happened?"

"There was a letter. From Rovinj."

This time, I had to swallow. Hell. "Irina, not from—?"

"From Hugo."

And she told me about the letter and the stamps and the handwriting she had recognized instantly, and how she had immediately thought that . . . But the letter had been addressed to Anna, and so of course she couldn't . . . So, for a while, she thought that perhaps it was just . . . But when Anna acted so strangely, she thought that . . . Anna insisted she hadn't read the letter yet, but Irina was sure she . . . And even more so when Anna suddenly . . .

Then she started sobbing a bit, and I felt upset, too.

"Pierre?" Her voice was barely audible.

"Yes?"

"What now?"

"Are you thinking what I'm thinking?"

"Of course I'm thinking what you think. What else?"

All right, we thought the same thing! People who are quarreling can easily think the same thing, can't they? For once, I was not confused.

Of course we both thought of Michael. Her son, my stepson. Our son, said Irina. So, yes, our son. Croatia. Anna's brother. Well, half-brother. Brother, said Anna. So, yes, brother.

"Pierre?"

"Yes?"

"Look after her, won't you."

"Of course, of course."

"She took the seven-fifty-seven. So she should be there about ten."

"I'm home."

"Thank you."

"Don't mention it." (Polite, polite!)

Then she hung up.

I went to stand by the window again. The sun was higher

in the sky and a yellow stripe was already visible on the gray sand of the beach. I could see the shadow of my own building moving to the right, and I checked my watch.

Nine-fourteen, I read, thinking about Hugo.

Why hadn't I said anything about Hugo? Why hadn't I told Irina that Hugo was here, in Ostend, for his Sunset Festival? Why hadn't I told her I had just been talking to Hugo on the phone about the casino? My casino project?

Shit, I said to myself, shit, shit, shit! I relit the last half of my cigar. It tasted like a dirty ashtray.

I was screwing things up once again.

Jonas I had lost, Michael had slipped away from me, and with Irina things had gone thoroughly wrong. Which left Anna. There was only Anna left.

The temperature was going up, I could feel it. The sun was blazing. I stared out over the sea and thought about what I was going to cook. What did she like? Something Mediterranean, I thought. Scampi, fresh garlic, olive oil, couscous. I had to go shopping urgently. I had about an hour.

Anna

A town by the sea

I examined the card again and took a deep breath. It didn't necessarily mean anything. My father lived in a building with more than sixty apartments. This could be sheer coincidence. But it could just as well not be coincidence. I pushed the card into the back pocket of my jeans and stepped out of the train.

When I saw a boy waiting on one of the seats on the platform, I felt confused. He stood up when he saw me. He had a swimmer's broad shoulders, his dark blond, curly hair was cut short, he wore a pale blue cotton V-neck sweater, worn-out brown jeans, and dirty running shoes. He looked like Bert. Which wasn't all that surprising, because it was Bert. On top of everything else!

I should have walked straight on, cut him dead, or told him off then and there, whatever, done something definite, but I didn't. As if in slow motion, I could feel myself walk up to him.

"Hi."

"Hi."

He shoved his hands in his pockets and gave me a quick grin. I looked at him as coldly as I could.

"How did you know I was here?" Quick shrug. "You called my mother."

"Y-y-yes."

"Shit, Bert, we'd agreed—"

"I know, I know."

"But how did you get here so fast?" That quick shrug again.

"Hitched. Bit of luck. A guy with a Porsche. Steady ninety-nine, in the express lane. I was here at half past nine." He grinned once, looked down at the ground, and shifted from one foot onto the other.

Then he looked at me with one of those damp, doggy expressions, and something inside me began to melt.

"Come on," I said. "Let's go look at the water." I should never have done that!

We put our bags in a locker at the station, and soon we were walking along the wharf with the fishing boats; my hand under his sweater on his bare skin, the air warm, the breeze cool, gulls drifting above us, and all around us the air smelling of salt and the sea and fresh shrimps.

"What now?" he said, but I put my finger across his lips, pulled my finger away, and put my lips in its place. And so we stood for a long time with the gulls drifting, etcetera.

Perhaps people stopped to watch us as we stood there, perhaps they didn't, but for the moment I didn't care.

The harbor channel was broad and open to the sea. A catamaran was setting off for England, trailing a wake of foam and waves.

Bert gasped for breath, smiling uncertainly, and asked again, "And what now?"

I drew my tongue over his lips, looked at him quickly, one eye shut against the sun. "You can't help me," I said.

"But—"

"I have to do this on my own, Bert. This has nothing to do with you."

"That's what you said yesterday. But I really want to have something to do with it. I love—"

"Hey, we've split up, remember?"

"Correction: you've split up."

"Isn't that the same thing?"

"Well, it isn't for me!"

I knew it, I knew it. Anna and boys, it always went wrong. The usual miserable feeling started welling up in me.

It wasn't an overwhelming feeling, it wasn't really to do with what was happening right now, but I recognized it only too well. From years ago and from just recently. It brought a great coldness, it worked its way under my skin, it forced itself on me and nagged away at my whole body until in the end I could do nothing but pull my hand away from underneath Bert's sweater.

His look nearly made me cry, but I couldn't help it.

"Hey, Ann, what's the matter?" (Bert called me Ann, too. It made me feel even more like crying.)

I forced my tongue to speak. Anything.

"I can't explain, Bert. Just let me be. You can't understand this."

Suddenly Bert turned cold, too. It seemed contagious, that miserable feeling. And suddenly I couldn't stand him. He laughed meanly.

"Okay, okay, I'm too dumb, aren't I? Bert's too dumb to

understand. And Lady Anna, the superior Anna, suddenly doesn't need Bert any longer. You can use Bert when you want him and dump him when you want to be rid of him. Isn't that right?"

Just what we needed, a shitty remark like that. I felt even colder. The mere fact that he was standing here next to me was bad enough.

See? That feeling inside me nagged, See? You should never have spoken to him, you should never have gone with him, you should never have kissed him, because look: It's happening all over again, it's happening all over again.

I was furious with myself, so I started yelling at Bert. He yelled back, but I yelled even louder. I was much better at yelling than he was. More than likely, people stopped to watch us again, but I still didn't care.

When we finished, I felt absolutely terrible, a real bitch, but strangely enough we both stayed put.

Distraught, I looked at Bert, and distraught, he looked somewhere else. I couldn't explain it. A sickly scent blew across from the beach. Sunscreen, the first visitors of the season. Tourists. I started to feel sick. I swallowed. He pushed his hands deep inside the pockets of his brown jeans, looked at the pavement, then at the absent clouds.

Okay, he nodded. Okay.

Poor, dear Bert . . .

He came and stood very close to me, his hands still in his pockets, and rested his cheek against my throat and he smelled so lovely, of honest sweat and boy smells. I stroked his short sun-bleached curls, his cheek, his neck. I kissed his eyes, but the coldness did not go away.

"Hey, Bert . . ."

He nodded and shook his head. "Sorry," he muttered. "I'm so sorry . . ."

I shook my head, No, it's me, it's my fault. What am I doing to you? I am . . . I put my hand over his mouth, wanted to stroke his cheek again, but I couldn't.

"What are you going to do?" he asked.

"I have to go and visit my father. And then see—"

"—a friend, no doubt?"

"It isn't what you think. Hugo is—"

"Hugo? Hugo who?"

"Hugo Vandamme."

"Oh, him."

Quick alarm. Did Bert know anything about Hugo?

"Do you know Hugo Vandamme?"

"Only by name. The music, you know."

And he pointed listlessly at a poster on a lamppost. Sunset Festival. Of course, Hugo's festival. The poster showed a stylized orange sun with the names of the stars draped around it in a bluish fluorescent color. Hideous.

"So?" I asked.

"What?"

"Are you going to the festival?"

"Don't know. Tonight, perhaps. The opening concert. In the casino—"

"The casino? You sure?"

"Look." He pointed at the poster. Sunset Festival. Opening Concert, MS, Casino, 9 P.M., I read.

"What's MS?"

"Who. You should ask, *who's* MS? A singer. Frenchman. You know him, I'm sure."

I shook my head. "Means nothing to me."

"AIDS."

"What?" I thought I hadn't understood him properly.

"AIDS. The guy has AIDS. He's nearly dead. Good singer, though."

"Hang on. MS?"

"That's what he calls himself these days."

I stiffened. Of course I knew MS. MS stood for Mano Solo. The small, thin Frenchman with the Spanish name, with lyrics so sharp they seemed scratched into his own skin, and with the scream of life in his throat. Mano Solo didn't have AIDS, he *was* AIDS. From all the rooftops he shouted it around Europe: I have it, and I'm still alive. I am still *alive!* How he survived, I didn't know. Over the past two years he'd canceled more concerts than he had played, it seemed, but he was still alive. I hated him. Thin, dark, with fiery eyes, that's how he looked. "That guy looks a bit like Bowie when he was young," Bert said once when we were watching MTV. I had instantly zapped Mano Solo off the screen and shown Bert the door. "Hey, what's the matter this time, Ann?" but of course I hadn't replied, just stared at his back as he slouched off into the night, dejected. How could Bert have known that Jonas, too, looked like Bowie when he was young?

They were back again. First Michael, now Jonas. Mano Solo and the young Bowie.

Bert kept staring at that ugly poster, as if it contained some secret message. I shut my eyes and massaged my neck, which was stiff and sore, as if I had the flu.

I wanted to go home. I wanted to sit in the garden with my mother, eat tomatoes with mozzarella and chat about nothing much. I wanted to sit in a schoolroom doing a history exam and let Kristel copy my answers. I wanted a spicy-cookie sandwich in my lunch box. I wanted to sit in my room listening to Nick Cave. I wanted to hang around the school gate watching boys sputter past on their scooters, and joke about aftershave and panty liners. And watch American weepies with Mama late at night. I wanted to be at home.

But that was out of the question, because at home a letter from Istria had dropped into the mailbox, and at home my mother was thinking about the past, and so everybody was home now. Everyone and everything. Michael, and Jonas, and Dad, and the war, and AIDS. They were all there.

It was as if the millennium bug had already struck in my head. My thoughts were running out of control, and turning them back was impossible. *Do you want to restart the computer in MS-DOS mode? Sorry, wrong command. Error code ###.*

I opened my eyes and blinked in the fierce light. Bert looked at me in surprise.

"Hey, Ann?"

Tourists were wandering about, viewing the sea through binoculars. They were wearing shorts and loud summer shirts and Ray-Bans. Their calves were burned red, and they had plastic sandals on their swollen feet. A flock of seagulls circled a fishing boat as it was leaving the harbor.

I was at the beach. Anna was away from home. Anna was traveling. Anna had made friends on the train with a strange man with heart disease. Anna was on her way to her father's.

If things are in such a strange state, you might as well make a strange decision, I thought, and decided I wanted to go to that concert with Bert..

"Bert?"

He had followed the direction of my eyes and stood staring vacantly at those seagulls. He turned toward me, but I couldn't read his thoughts.

"What?"

"Have you got a ticket?"

He shrugged. No, in other words.

"Listen," I said. "Make sure you're at the casino entrance at half past eight. I'll be there. With two tickets. Okay?"

"Perhaps."

"Bert? Bert!"

But he had already turned and was walking away to the pier. I stood looking after him for a long time. Then I turned and started walking toward my father's apartment.

the
view of the sea
is free

It was quite close

It was quite close. Much sooner than I had expected, I stood eye to eye with a gigantic gray stone sailor, bare head bent, legs slightly apart, with his hands modestly crossed over his crotch.

"You can't miss it, Anna, it's near the monument for the drowned fishermen, a gigantic statue, totally tasteless, but easily recognizable."

"I'll find it, Dad."

Twelve Albertina Walk, apartment 6D. His new address. Under D in my address book, noted down months ago. When he . . . moved.

Via the elbow, the armpit, and the shoulders of the stone sailor, I looked up. It really was a very ugly statue, and the dark brown building in the background was a whole lot uglier still. Built in the fifties, I knew. A square stone facade with a lot of glass rectangles, and a human being hiding behind each rectangle.

"Those things are so unbelievably ugly, Anna, you've got no idea. Real monstrosities. But they do have a view of the sea, all of them . . ."

"Monstrosities," to him, meant blocks of apartments, concrete insults to the people who had to live in them. But he was quite happy to make an exception for the "monstrosities" by the sea, for the sake of the view. For behind that view of the sea there was a vision. He had explained it to me on the phone not long ago. And that vision, Anna, dates from the fifties, when some government, as if by a miracle, had an inspiration and decided that everyone, including the ordinary "working man," had a right to at least fifteen days of paid holidays, including an affordable view of the sea. And so, in those same fifties, under the approving eye of that magnanimous government, a large number of ugly but cheap buildings had been plonked down by the seawall. The sea belonged to everyone, and the view had to be affordable, even for ordinary working people, you understand, Anna?

Yes, yes, I understood.

And I should understand, too, that as an architect he was horrified by the ugliness of "those things," stupid Lego blocks just thrown together, but that as a person he was right behind that vision.

Yes, I understood that, too.

And now he lived in one of those Lego boxes himself.

Would he feel insulted? Or would he feel pleased with his free view?

I looked up along that ugly facade, counting the floors. 6D.

Somewhere on the sixth floor a window was open. Was that him? He knew I hated cigar smoke, so he was airing the apartment. It was possible.

But it could be someone else, too.

Perhaps it was Devolder; he lived here too, didn't he? Or perhaps it was someone else altogether, someone I didn't know, just a stranger? A random occupant of a random Lego block?

The wind tugged at my hair.

Even when there is no wind, it's breezy here. Always.

My hair was getting long again.

I closed my eyes, and the wind brought me the scents of a summer beach. Sunscreen mixed with sand, tourists' skin burned red, overly sweet waffles and ice cream, and, from a distance, the sweetish smell of children being sick. An image from the past rose up. A steaming hot traffic jam between Brussels and Ostend, and I was on the backseat, my plastic sick bag at the ready. Carsick, as always. Sigh.

I took a deep breath, crossed the street past the stone sailor, and pushed open the glass door.

In the large, empty hall I found a big panel of doorbells. There was no name next to 6D. After two rings, there was a response. His voice sounded hollow and metallic through the intercom.

"Elevator on the right, sixth floor."

Hello, Dad!

I was alone in the elevator. It smelled of cheap perfume. He was waiting for me on the landing. Behind him an open door. Ugly dark brown, mass produced, with a peephole.

"Hello, Dad."

"Anna! Come in, come in!" he said cheerfully. As if I was some remote cousin who had come to tea. He bent toward me, and I kissed him on the cheek. He didn't look well, and that wasn't just because he hadn't shaved.

He turned and walked ahead of me into the hall. Ugly dark brown floor covering, faded wallpaper with a dark brown flower pattern. There was a tobacco smell around (more dark brown). To my right there was an open door; I looked through it to see if there was an open window, but I couldn't see from where I was.

He pointed to a coat stand in a corner.

"You could put your bags there for the moment—" but then he noticed I didn't have any luggage and said, "Oh." I muttered something about having left it at the station and picking it up later, and having gone for a bit of a walk by the sea. "Oh," he said again, quickly adding that I didn't have to explain why I was a bit late, of course not, what an idea, but that he had been sort of wondering, you know, not that it mattered, and not that he had been worried, not at all, but, you know, these days, with those trains, you just never knew. . . . Yes, sorry, I said, and perhaps I should have rung, let him know I would be a bit late, but no, no explanations needed, he answered quickly, we had plenty of time, didn't we?

Yes, yes, we had plenty of time.

And then we stood there, and neither of us could think of anything to say.

"Thirsty?" he asked suddenly.

"What?"

"Are you thirsty? Would you like a drink? Fruit juice?"

"Yes, yes, and yes." I grinned.

He laughed, relaxed a little. "I'll see what I've got."

He disappeared into the kitchen, and I walked into what

I supposed was the living room, but I stopped in the doorway. I remembered this room, and I shouldn't be there. Prohibited area, Anna!

It was his workroom in Holsbeek. I recognized his angled drawing desk, his black desk lamp, and his Swedish chair. His architecture books stacked on the floor, the bundles of papers in suspension files, the plans and sketches spread out on tables and chairs hastily pushed together, Polaroids of building sites pinned to the walls with drawing pins, a model on a stool with a torch next to it to test the angle of the light, his crystal ashtray full of brown cigar butts . . .

I walked in, hesitantly, as if I was still scared of being caught. In the center of the room I stopped, looked around, nodded. Obviously he had, bit by bit, moved his whole workroom here. All his things. And I had hardly even noticed. What on earth had kept my head so busy this past year? And at the same time I thought what I had already been thinking two days ago: It doesn't really make a great deal of difference whether he lives on the coast or not. Suddenly I was seized by a kind of homesickness for that room in Holsbeek, which always smelled of cigars; that mysterious workroom of his, which I wasn't allowed to enter as a little girl.

Annoyed, I swallowed my sadness. Grow up, Anna! You've known this for a long time! Your father is living on the coast, *so what?*

One of the walls was really special. It was completely covered in ancient blueprints, attached with drawing pins.

They were obviously from an era before computers, because they were hand-drawn and the many annotations were written with a nib pen, in a stylish, old-fashioned script with lots of curly flourishes. They made me think of plans for an intergalactic spaceship from *Star Wars* or something, because they represented a futuristic kind of building, a perfect semicircle, gigantic, with all sorts of rooms and command posts.

"Beautiful, isn't it?"

He was standing next to me. I jumped. Sprung. I pointed at the blueprints.

"Is this it?"

He nodded. "The casino. These are the original plans, from the fifties."

"No monstrosity, if you ask me."

"Oh, no. Here you are." He handed me a glass. "Apple juice is all I've got. Not from the fridge, I'm afraid."

"That's fine."

It tasted like yogurt diluted with water.

"Look," he said. "This design is pure genius. It follows the curve in the seawall perfectly. It was Couperus who said—"

"Who?"

"Couperus. A writer. He stayed here a hundred years ago. He wrote, 'In an arc of perfect grace, the seawall curves against the sea and the sky.' The architect understood perfectly."

"A round casino?"

"Semicircular, to be exact, and—" Then a lengthy account

of that brilliant design by that brilliant architect, of the disappointing result (endless compromises, you know what politics are like), and of the present local authority who had finally decided to do something about it. . . . I thought it was a great story.

Suddenly he went over to the window, dragged the curtains aside, and opened the window wide. "Come and have a look."

I stood next to him.

"If you lean out the window—careful!—you can see it. To your left. Far left. You have to look close along the wall."

Yes, I could see it. A curved building, glass and concrete, gray like a bunker, just visible in a bend of the seawall. The semicircle of the blueprints.

"Is that scaffolding all around it?"

"That's just the start of the restoration work. The side facing the sea is very badly decayed. The real work hasn't started yet."

"It looks like a bunker."

He nodded. "That's right," he said. "And I think that's what the architect intended. There have been two wars here, you know. But as far as I'm concerned, it's going to become a bunker with a sea view." And he launched into another long explanation of his proposals, which would completely reinstate the original architect's plans. The theater and concert hall would be moved to the inland side, while facing the sea, there would be extensive spaces for . . .

"Dad?"

"Yes?"

I was happy to see my father happy, that he was pleased with his work and so on, and I really rather liked old buildings myself, but for the moment I'd had enough. I had something to ask him.

"Do you know a guy called Devolder?"

He looked startled.

"Devolder? No, not that I can think of. Who is he?"

"Middle-aged, a bit older than you. Very tall and thin. Bald, big nose, old-fashioned clothes, three-piece suit—"

"Doesn't ring a bell, no. Why?"

The phone rang. Dad answered. Still the same old cordless phone above his drawing table.

"Bracke." His voice immediately sounded different. "Oh, hello. What? Yes, she's here. How did you know? . . . Oh, yes, I see . . . Yes, I'll put her on."

I'd already guessed who it was. My father covered the mouthpiece with his hand.

"Hugo, for you."

I nodded, took the phone from him. For a moment he stood there with a questioning look, but then he disappeared into the kitchen.

"Hugo?"

"Hello, little monster."

I smiled despite myself.

"Hello, prickly beard."

"I'm glad you're here."

"Me too, Hugo," I said after the briefest hesitation.

"Listen, I'm terribly sorry to spring this on you, but I've really got very little time. Can you be here in half an hour or so, at the festival office? I've got something for you."

"The festival office? Where's that?"

"In the casino. Go through the stage door and ask for me at reception."

"Oh, Hugo—" I looked over my shoulder. I could see Dad standing at the sink. He lifted the lid off a saucepan, then moved back from the escaping steam with a curse.

"Yes?" said Hugo.

I lowered my voice. "Do you know any more?"

"What?"

"Have you got any more news?"

Silence.

"Oh, you mean, my letter. . . . I should never have written that." He sighed, like someone gasping for breath. "Yes, I have more news. I, um . . . well, I've got something to show you."

"What?"

"Come to the festival office. I'll show you."

"Okay." I tried to sound casual. "See you in half an hour."

"Okay, see you."

He hung up, and I put down the receiver very carefully, the way I used to at the time of my first boyfriends, when my parents were not to know how long and how late I had been on the phone. I walked down the passage to the kitchen, and that took a long time, because I came across the photo on the way. That photo. It was pinned to the wall with four drawing pins, among the dark brown flowers. Just as in Holsbeek, it was hanging next to the kitchen door, and it still showed a white tear across the middle, between my two brothers.

Was it really a tear between life and death?

I went into the kitchen and stood next to my father by the sink. There was a smell like scorched Ping-Pong balls.

"Hm, I think I've—" he said.

"Don't worry," I said. The seagulls were flying very low. We could see them from where we stood, floating past the window, like on a wide-screen TV. He followed my glance.

"Storm," he said. "When they fly low like that, there's a storm coming. Definitely."

"Yes," I replied, and for a moment my thoughts drifted away with the gulls. Those birds are supposed to be able to soar on the wind for six miles without once flapping their wings. Real acrobats. As seen on *National Geographic*.

". . . set the table?"

"Sorry. What were you saying, Dad?"

"I said the food was ready, and shall I set the table?"

"Oh, no," I said quickly.

"No?"

I put on a sad face and muttered that, you know, I had to leave urgently, an appointment, you see, and I really appreciated him cooking for me. Couscous even, but really . . .

He smiled rather bitterly. "An appointment, hm?"

I felt myself blushing, and he said quickly that of course it was none of his business, and that of course he understood, but because I really liked couscous he'd thought that . . . but put off isn't lost . . . and there's another day tomorrow, isn't there . . . because I was going to stay a few days, wasn't I? Yes, yes, of course, I stammered, but . . .

Ah well, I'd screwed up again, I had disappointed him once more, bad timing from beginning to end, Anna. I felt so rotten and confused I didn't know what to say, and of course he misunderstood my silence, thinking it was all his fault, that he had screwed up again, and so he was silent too. Just as half an hour ago (or was it an hour?), we stood together in the hall, embarrassed like two self-conscious teenagers. Finally, I grabbed the door handle.

"Well, I'd better go, Dad."

He sort of loitered by the kitchen door, next to the torn photo, and I had no earthly idea what he was thinking. Perhaps he knew much more than I thought, or just as likely he was simply wondering what color socks to put on tomorrow.

"See you later, Dad."

"Um . . . Anna?"

"Yes?"

"I did know a Devolder once."

"Did you really?" I let go of the door handle, turning toward him.

"A very long time ago."

"And?"

"He was a doctor. A very good one, actually. But I don't think you . . . I mean, you were still . . ."

"Too young, I suppose? Far too little?" I blurted it out

before I realized, and it sounded nastier than I meant it to. Much nastier.

He stiffened. "Yes," he said curtly, and pursed his lips. I knew what that meant. End of conversation. No point insisting further.

I cursed myself. Shit, Anna, you've done it again! What's gotten into you? When are you going to learn? I didn't know where to look.

He shoved his hands into his pockets, he might even have clenched his fists, but suddenly he fished out a key. He came over to me quickly and pressed the key into my hand. Here, in case it gets late. My room was the second door on the left, the bed was made. I nodded. Thanks, Dad. Yes. Bye. See you later.

When the glass door closed behind me, I had to screw up my eyes against the sun. It was nearly midday. The stone sailor stood motionless, his hands crossed over his crotch, the gulls circling round his head. I looked up along the square facade, and saw that more windows were now open. I wondered which one was Devolder's. On the sixth floor, I saw a curtain being shut.

It was quite a walk

It was quite a walk to the casino, and it wasn't much fun.

I had intended to be furious with Hugo. Over breakfast I'd dreamed up some pretty nasty opening lines, and on the train I'd called him everything under the sun in my mind, Mr. Hugo Vandamme with his cowardly ways. Now, during the long walk along the Ostend seawall, I was trying to get my ideas clear: You're a loathsome individual, Hugo! A creep, a coward, a disgrace! How dare you write me a letter like that! And so on.

Well, that was a spectacular failure.

I was angry, sure, but not with Hugo. I was furious with myself. I raged, but at myself. Bloody hell, Anna, when are you ever going to learn? You've screwed up again! Grow up! For a start, learn to have a conversation. An ordinary conversation, you know, somebody says something and you reply without instantly causing havoc with some stupid, sorry-ass, juvenile remark like you just did at your dad's place!

In a word, my head was buzzing, but not with Hugo. I marched along the seawall, feeling more and more depressed, thinking about my father, about our totally failed reunion, the missed opportunity (yet another one). I also thought about Daniel Devolder, who had worked himself into my head and was showing no signs of leaving.

To add to my misery, the whole area around the casino had been turned into some sort of war zone. Everywhere I was faced with barriers, gates, heaps of rubble and sand, concrete mixers, holes in the ground, tall fences, yellow-and-black tapes, and orange flashing lights. The whole country seemed to be turning into a building site. I had to detour through at least five streets, and got pretty lost. And by the time I finally reached the casino, at the wrong entrance of course, I had long since forgotten all the things I was going to throw at Hugo.

Festival reception: arrow pointing to the right, next door, please. Finally.

"Hugo Vandamme, please?"

The guy at the counter pointed to a staircase. "Level 2B. Look for a phone. Fifty-fifty chance Hugo'll be on it."

On level 2B there were lots of people sitting around smoking cigarettes, staring at computer monitors, shouting into cell phones, munching rolls. So that's how you organize a festival. "Hugo? No, haven't seen him. You seen Hugo? No, you haven't either? Try the basement. Hugo likes plumbing the depths." Laughter. Thank you, ladies and gentlemen.

More stairs, more gray concrete corridors with numbered doors. It was like being on the *Titanic,* third class.

I finally located him in an almost deserted basement bar, way below sea level, behind an espresso, and with a cell phone clamped to his ear. Look for a phone, and you'll find Hugo.

He raised an index finger when he saw me, cut his

conversation short—"Got to go, Jacob"—and put his cell phone down on the table. His face was radiant. He came over and threw his arms around me. It got to me, despite everything.

"Hey, little monster," he whispered over my right shoulder. "You've no idea how pleased I am to see you."

"Me too, Hugo," I said, and meant it. What had I wanted to say to him?

Then he pushed me away, his arms outstretched, his hands on my shoulders. He looked me over, shook his head and grinned crookedly. "You look great!"

He had huge bags under his eyes, he looked deathly pale in the dull neon light, his goatee had turned a mousy gray, and his hair had been cropped really short, but I still told him he looked great too.

"You're a good liar," he said.

"Yes, I am."

He laughed too loudly. I recognized that laugh, but it sounded a bit hollow against the concrete of the basement bar.

"Just a sec," he said and turned toward someone I hadn't noticed in the half dark. "Karen?"

"Yes, Hugo?"

An Irish-looking beauty, with long, reddish curls, wearing a loose, half-transparent dress. She was his assistant, judging by the way he spoke to her.

"I'm going up to the loft now, to get changed. I'll be unavailable for a while."

"Okay, Hugo," said Karen. She nodded at me with raised eyebrows, granting me a cool smile. To her it was obvious: Her boss was going off with some young thing, and she was being left to do the dirty work.

"Come on," Hugo said to me. "We haven't got much time."

I felt a bit sorry for Karen, so I gave her a broad, helpless sort of smile. She smiled back, a bit surprised, but she obviously would just as soon have given me the finger.

Meanwhile Hugo was dragging me along to the elevator.

"We have to be quick," he insisted. "It's the opening concert tonight, and we're having problems with—"

"MS, isn't it?"

"Yes. Fantastic opener, don't you think?"

"How is he these days?"

Hugo raised his eyebrows.

"Good, I think, good. I mean it. He's in his hotel room. Sleeping."

"That's good," I said.

We were interrupted by the elevator, which took us to the parking lot. Hugo held the door open for me, raving about his car. Something American with lots of chrome and big fins, pink like a Barbie doll's dress. "Nineteen-fifty-nine Chevrolet," Hugo said, proud as a peacock. Wow.

A bit later, stuck in a traffic jam, he returned to the topic of MS. Mano Solo.

"I really love that guy," he said. "Fantastic artist. Not just for his music. For what he is."

"For what he is?"

"*Yes,*" he said emphatically. "For the way he's handling his illness." He turned his head to me. "And, *yes*, because he reminds me of Jonas."

The city traffic was mayhem. From left and right, hostile steel beasts loomed at us, coming terrifyingly close, like armored vehicles in a war film. Hugo lowered his window to hurl abuse at the advancing Nazis. Then he looked at me apologetically. "People and their cars—"

You mean boys and their toys, I thought.

"It's the stress," he said, and proceeded to whine about lack of freedom, and frustration, and the meaning of existence.

"You sound like you're having your midlife crisis," I said. I figured he must be thirty-two.

"Believe it or not, but I think a lot about Jonas," he said.

That wasn't quite what I'd meant, but I responded anyway. "Still?"

"Like you," he nodded.

Not true, I wanted to say, but bit my lip, because it was true.

"And Michael?" I asked rather curtly.

"Shit. The bridge," he groaned, letting go of the steering wheel. The Chevrolet stood still, and suddenly everything went quiet. All around us, engines were switched off, and then the bridge started rising, agonizingly slowly, until it towered high above the houses, like the threatening finger of God in the flawless blue sky.

And a boat glided past. I watched, breathless. Just an

ordinary, small yacht it was, with only its mast and snow-white sail visible, but it had an almost unearthly beauty. A boat in the city. A mast and a sail sliding past, oblivious of the chaos, the agitation and irritation of the city traffic. All the sweating, the abuse, the despair, the rage, the whole noisy, smelly traffic jam, the exhaust fumes—the hectic rhythm of the city failed to have any impact. There was only the water, the wind, the bridge, and a few gulls. Hugo leaned back in his seat. He shrugged his shoulders, looking at me with an almost embarrassed smile.

"I actually rather like living here," he said.

"Do you live here now?"

"During the festival. At a friend's place. This guy's a photographer, and he's almost always away covering some event somewhere. He's in Kosovo right now, I think. Still trouble there. He's got a loft."

Photographer? Kosovo? Loft?

Hugo gave a little cough.

"And, you know, about Michael—"

"Didn't you say you had something for me?"

"In the loft, yes. Hang on . . ."

Suddenly, car horns were hooting behind us. The signal. The bridge was being lowered, so the great migration could continue and the traffic began to move again. Hugo shifted gears angrily, shouted something through his window, and with a roar we shot forward. Quiet, Anna. Look straight ahead and say nothing. Breathe slowly. From the left I heard sighs, curses from the right, roaring engines on all sides. Like tanks, or race cars at the starting line. A traffic jam needs to move. Next to me, Hugo sat tapping the steering wheel. Finally, the bridge was back to horizontal above the mirror-flat water, and we moved smoothly across. Hugo accelerated, steered the Chevrolet through a few desolate curves, and with a squeal of tires like in a bad cop movie, we stopped in front of a redbrick building in the docklands.

I looked around. We were close to the old blue-and-white-striped lighthouse. I recognized it. I had just been able to see it from Dad's flat. From a distance I heard the shouts of children playing.

"Coming?"

Hugo stood waiting by the gate of the redbrick building. A warehouse of some sort, by the looks of it. On the facade, large flaking letters spelled HUNGARIA.

"Is this it?"

"Come on."

He walked under a tall gateway and into a gigantic goods elevator, pulling the grating shut with a clatter. I felt like a miner going down into the pit, but we were going up. Third floor.

The loft, as you might expect, was extremely spacious, stylish, and sparsely decorated, with a smooth concrete floor, bare brick walls, steel-framed windows. The few pieces of furniture could either be fiercely expensive or from the Salvation Army. One window faced the bypass, which was barely a couple of hundred yards away—the pylons were exactly three stories high, so the traffic was at eye level—another looked out on an old rail track (to the docks,

I guessed) with grass growing between the rails, and a third window stood open to the sea. Cars, trains, boats. It was like a major traffic junction. All we need now is a plane, I thought, and sure enough, that very instant there was the thundering roar of a transport plane flying immediately above us. The windows rattled.

"That's the only disadvantage of this place," said Hugo. "We're directly under the flight path of the main runway. A drink?"

The fridge was gigantic. It looked like a cross between a space shuttle and a soft drink vending machine.

"No, thanks."

Hugo got himself a bottle of Corona and with a sigh dropped onto a couch. He rubbed his neck, his eyes shut.

"Tired?" I sat on the couch opposite him and dropped my camera bag by my feet.

He nodded. "Rovinj, then Vienna, and now this here. I've slept about three hours a night the last few months."

I waited, listening to the sounds from outside.

The traffic was so constant that its distant roar made a new kind of silence. A hum between your ears. A train somewhere. Strange—wasn't there grass growing between the rails? Another plane passed overhead, a bit farther away this time. In the silence of its dying roar I heard vague harbor noises, clanging, like hammers hitting steel plates, and the ponderous grinding sound of cranes. A fishing boat drifted past the third window, and for a moment I thought I could hear the quiet putting of its diesel engine.

"Tell me about Rovinj, Hugo."

Still with his eyes closed, he sucked in air and expelled it through puffed-up cheeks. "I should never have written to you."

"So you said."

"Did I?"

Another silence full of sounds.

Abruptly, Hugo sat up and leaned forward, elbows on knees, folding his hands in front of his mouth.

"After my . . . meeting with Marta, I stayed in Rovinj for another two days. I went to the town hall, the registry office, called a lot of hotels, called the consulate, faxed the Interior Ministry in Zagreb, called a few Croatian friends, asking them to make inquiries here and there. I even faxed Marta's aunt—"

"In Italy?"

"Yes. Do you know her?"

"Jelena Markovic. I've heard her name. Mom still rings her occasionally. How come you know her?"

"I met her at Michael's, in the summer of '94 or '95—" He stopped midsentence and looked at me. I noticed how red his eyes were. "Do you really want to know all this, Anna?" As if he hoped I didn't.

"What did you say?" I thought I hadn't understood him properly.

"I mean, for all these years you've refused to hear anything at all, and so—"

"What was that you said, Hugo?" It was as if he'd hit me in the face. I could feel the blood rush to my cheeks, and I burst out, "Want to? Refused! You bloody coward! As if it's up to me to want or to refuse! For years I didn't want to hear anything, yes, that's right! Nothing about Michael, nothing about Jonas! Nothing about the past, that was the agreement! The agreement with my parents, and with you, too, because 'the past,' Hugo, 'the past' was nothing but misery, sickness, and death, and false hopes, and I'd had that up to here! And my parents . . . no, let's leave them out of this. After all, you didn't write to them, did you, Hugo? Because you were too much of a coward. It was me you wrote to, Hugo! And why me? Why Anna? Oh, but Anna, she's young! Anna, she's tough! Anna, she's the one who can 'give this past some sort of future.' That's what you wrote, wasn't it? Beautifully put, Hugo, so moving. Lump in the throat stuff, ha ha! Bloody hell, Hugo, this letter of yours, if only you knew what I— Here! See for yourself!" And, hands shaking with anger, I waved the screwed-up, half-burned, torn-up, and stuck-back-together rag of paper in his face. He winced.

"Yes, Hugo, just look! Screwed up, torn up, nearly burned. I tried hard to destroy it, to make it disappear. But I couldn't manage. I wanted to, but I couldn't do it! And you knew perfectly well that I wouldn't be able to. Admit it, Hugo: You knew that when you sent it. And so, my friend, cut the crap! Don't come at me with those slimy half-baked questions, pretending you want to spare me the rest of the misery, because it's too late for that. Because, ever since that letter, you bastard, *it's not up to me to want anything!*"

There. I'd said it.

I went over to the window and looked out at the sea. Another boat glided past, one of those stupid tour boats, decked out in little colored flags. The metallic whine of an amplified voice echoed over the water and just got to me. Behind me there was silence.

Then Hugo cleared his throat and said softly, "That was a stupid question. Sorry."

Sure was! A very stupid question!

"You're right, you don't have a choice. Any more than I did when I sent that letter."

"Oh, really? Explain."

"Just think about it," he said to my back. "Would you ever send a letter like that to your father? Or your mother?"

I bit my lip. He had a point. No, of course not. I'd already worked that one out myself, on the train.

"Could I have not written at all?"

I'd thought about that, too. In my room, the day before yesterday. Of course that wasn't possible. Absolutely not. Shit, shit, shit. He's thought this through in exactly the same way as me. No way out.

"Believe me, you were the only possibility. Otherwise, I would never have done it."

Abruptly, I turned toward him. He turned round, too, and for a moment we looked straight into each other's eyes. Then I turned back to the window. There was a crack in the glass. I bit my lip even harder. Wishing it would bleed.

I was the only possibility. I swallowed hard, then said, "Hugo?"

"Yes?"

"That red felt pen of Jonas's, what exactly was that all about?"

He laughed, a brief, dry laugh.

"Censorship, of course! In his letters from America, he often told me things the family in Holsbeek weren't supposed to know. He marked those with a red felt pen in the margin: '*Top secret!* Definitely not to be passed on to Holsbeek! My parents must not know about this!'"

"What sort of things?"

"What do you think? Wild nights, money problems, secret things. . . . Do you tell your parents everything about your boyfriends and what you get up to with them?"

I shrugged.

"But when he fell ill, the red felt pen became really serious, of course. This was genuinely *classified*, literally a deadly silence."

He was quiet again.

"How long had you actually known he had AIDS?"

"April '90 is when he told us."

I was shocked. "Us?"

"Michael and me."

I turned. He had taken his glasses off and rubbed his eyes.

"That long? Three years before my parents?"

Hugo put his glasses back on and nodded. "Can you imagine, Anna? Three years of that red felt pen? Even now, my stomach cramps when I think of it. In every letter

I opened, there they were again, thick red marks in the margins. 'Don't tell Holsbeek, Hugo! My parents mustn't know anything!' And so I would ring Michael in Italy: what should we do? What could we do?"

"So, Michael knew, too—"

"Michael and I were the only ones to get letters like that. Eventually, his felt pen ran out. 'I'm not buying another one,' he wrote."

Michael, too. I could feel my pulse hammering in my head. "And now? Do they know it all now?"

"Not officially. Of course, they have their suspicions. That the three of us kept things from them. They knew how close I was to Jonas. And Michael."

"And now me."

"Yes." He smiled, a tired smile.

I thought about this. Holsbeek had their suspicions. What did Mom suspect? And my father?

"But why are you doing it all over again, man? I mean, if you hated that red felt pen so much, why are you using it again with me? Don't you know how much misery Jonas caused with his red pen?"

He looked me straight in the eyes again, coughed. "There's just one small difference, Ann."

Suddenly, he was calling me Ann. I liked that.

"What?"

"That time, I was hiding death. This time, I'm hiding life."

I stared at him, astounded. Oh, Anna! You incredibly selfish child! You've been spared everything. You may not have asked for it, but that's the truth. I felt as if I was on my bike, slowly sliding down a muddy slope, with nothing there to steady me.

Put my life next to my brother Michael's life. I had been spared everything. My parents had spared me as long as they could. Had they been right or wrong? Who was I to cast blame? And who was I to blame Hugo? *Hugo?*

Hugo sat with his head in his hands, his shoulders shaking as if he was suddenly very cold. I wrenched myself away from the window and went over to him. I stood close to him. For a moment, my hand drifted in the air—I hesitated, I was sixteen, and I hadn't ever seen an adult man cry. Could I comfort him? I put my hand on his shoulder.

He muttered all sorts of things, I couldn't understand him at first.

"Oh hell, Ann," he said. "Believe me, I tried . . . If anybody ever tried . . . Michael was my best friend, my blood brother."

I believed him. Of course I believed him, and I listened to him.

"Oh hell," he said over and over again. "I tried to stop him. 'You? Going there?' I said to him. 'And whose side d'you think you'll be on? Michael, tell me it's not true! You're not fool enough to become a nationalist!' He was offended. 'Shit, Vandamme, who do you take me for? Milosevic?'"

"Milosevic?" I said, shocked. "Was he there already at that time?"

"Of course he was there already! Milosevic has always been there. Milosevic has been there since 1980, when Tito died! Milosevic is the cleverest bastard of them all! And Michael knew that perfectly well."

"And even so?"

"Yes. And even so Michael went. 'Believe me, Vandamme,' he said. 'I'm not a Croatian, not a Serb, not a nationalist. Nationalism is the most stupid of all diseases, and I'm *not* sick, Vandamme, don't you understand? You know me better than that. And yet I have to go. It's my country, and I have to go and work there. I've got to do something, and that's where I have to do it.'"

"And so it was UNICEF?"

Hugo nodded. "He did great work there, but that's not the point. Remedying post-traumatic stress disorder was what it was called officially. Playing the clarinet for refugees is what Jonas once called it, sarcastically. And you must admit we were all a bit sarcastic at times about Michael, who absolutely had to go and save the world, over there, in his ex-country, and who had to go and play the hero. But to teach children who had been through a war to sing again, to help them get over it . . . Really beautiful work. Hats off . . . And I mean that, Ann."

"Yes, I know, Hugo. But there's more, isn't there?"

Yes, he nodded, there was more.

There was a Land Rover that hit a mine, three years ago. There had been a Red Cross message, people had died, but some of those dead apparently weren't all that dead. Isn't that right, Hugo? Hugo? Come on, help me along a bit! One single letter you've written to me, about a ravishing woman with flaxen hair, who was dancing at a pop festival, very much alive. You've got to give me more than that. Now! I don't have a choice anymore? So be it, but then I want to know. Now, Hugo.

"Weren't you going to show me something?"

He snapped his fingers, took a deep breath, and sprang to his feet. He went over to a metal bookshelf, and from among the books—photo books, I saw, Bill Brandt, Cartier-Bresson—he produced a large brown envelope.

"Here," he said.

I shivered when I saw the stamps. *Republika Hrvatska*. The letter was addressed to me.

Anna Bracke c/o Hugo Vandamme
Warmoesstraat 96
1000 Brussels

But Hugo's home address in Brussels had been crossed out and replaced with that of the Sunset Festival.

"I have my mail sent on during the festival. Have a look at the back."

I turned the envelope over and stared at the sender. The letters began to jump before my eyes. Perhaps it was the writing, which was uneven and hastily written in blue ball-point letters.

Marta c/o Sanja Paljutek
Hebrangova 18
1000 Zagreb
Croatia

"Marta?"

"Michael's Marta," he said, sounding as if he couldn't believe it either. Still.

I swallowed. My throat was as dry as the inside of a vacuum cleaner. "I wouldn't mind something to drink now," I said.

Hugo didn't react immediately.

"Hugo? Have you got anything to drink?"

"To drink? Oh, yes, of course!"

Suddenly, he was standing by the fridge, swinging the door open wildly.

"There's fruit juice, soda water—"

"Same as you."

"Didn't know you drank beer."

"I don't."

"I see." He ripped the cap off the bottle; the beer fizzed. "Cheers, little monster."

"Cheers, prickly beard."

It tasted bitter and strong, it tingled on my tongue and went down my throat much too fast. I choked, gasped for breath, and my eyes filled with tears.

"Good, isn't it?" said Hugo.

My head started to spin a bit. "Terrific," I groaned. "Okay, you idiot, where were we?"

"Marta," he said.

The envelope.

"When did this get here?"

"Yesterday."

I tried to decipher the postmark. June 10, 1999. I looked

at Hugo. He nodded. "She posted it the day after we met in Rovinj. It got here in rather a roundabout way."

"It came from Zagreb."

"The address is in Zagreb, but look at the postmark."

It was hard to read, but clear enough: Rovinj. That meant Marta had been in Rovinj at least one day after she bumped into Hugo.

"Does she know your address?"

"Michael certainly did, anyway. I moved to Brussels in April '96. I sent my new address to everybody, including Michael."

"In Fiesole?"

"Yes. That was just before he moved out of his apartment there. He and Marta were already living in ex-Yugoslavia more than in Italy. First in Celje, a small town in Slovenia, then Sarajevo, if I remember rightly. After that, there was just one more letter from them, in September. From Sarajevo. Just before the, um, accident."

My head was spinning. September '96, letter from Sarajevo. June '99, letter from Rovinj. I stared at the envelope in my hand.

"Aren't you going to open it?" Hugo asked.

"Of course."

There was nothing for it. I took a deep breath and tore the envelope open with my index finger. It felt as if I was doing something illegal. Hugo looked on over my shoulder, but his face clouded suddenly.

"Oh, shit!" He looked at his watch, had a sort of a fit, and started running about like a maniac.

"Hugo?"

"I should have been back ages ago! Shit, shit, shit!"

He trotted from the wardrobe to the bed, from the bed to the wardrobe, and disappeared behind a partition. I could hear water running, and a few seconds later he reappeared, a toothbrush in his mouth, foam on his lips.

"Liften—" He pulled the toothbrush out of his mouth. "Listen, I can reserve you some tickets for tonight, but you have to tell me now if you're coming. Yes? Yes. How many do you want? One, two, four? Two? Okay, two. Make sure you're there by quarter past eight, otherwise the tickets will be sold." He disappeared behind the partition again, and reappeared two seconds later in tight black pants, trying to simultaneously button up a pearly white lace shirt and wriggle his feet into black patent leather shoes. He managed all that. He threw a shiny black jacket over his arm, kissed me quickly, and rushed to the elevator. As the grille clanked shut, he called, "When you leave, just pull the gate shut behind you. And don't forget to close the windows. They've forecast a thunderstorm."

Then the elevator went down, I saw his hand wave above the floor, and he was gone. Everything went quiet. Bye-bye, Hugo.

In a daze I stared at the elevator shaft. He was gone. Did he really have to leave so urgently? Right then? And what about Marta's letter? Didn't he want to know what she'd written? Or was he abandoning me again, the swine? Would I have to cope on my own again?

Now, Anna! Stop! Don't get angry, not now. Not again. Hugo must have his reasons. Or at least . . . Oh, forget it.

I went back to the couch, weighing the envelope in my hand. That's something I always do with a letter. This was a heavy one. Then I slid my fingers inside the envelope and pulled out a thick bundle of paper. First I found a bunch of poor-quality photocopies. Grainy photos, gray text. I had a cursory look. They were articles from French, Italian, and English newspapers. They were all about the war in that ex-country. From '92 till now. From Bosnia to Kosovo. Most of the texts were by Marta, but the most recent ones were signed with the initials SP. SP? I examined the envelope: *Marta c/o Sanja Paljutek*. SP. Who was this Sanja? A friend of Marta's?

Okay, worry about that later, I decided. Because there was a letter, too.

Jumpy writing, the hurriedly written characters almost lost on a huge, white page. *Dearest Anna*, I read, and suddenly my eyes were full of tears. Hello, Marta. Long time no see.

I took a deep breath and read on.

Rovinj, June 10, 1999

Dearest Anna,
Sorry if I write mistakes in Dutch. I hardly speak it these days, and write it even less.

This is what I want to tell you—terrible things have happened, but I'm okay now. Please, call me at this number: 385-1-410757.

That's the address where I stay when I'm in Zagreb. Is a friend's place.

Don't wait too long. I must tell you something important. Don't say anything to your parents. Not yet. I won't call you, I'll wait for you. Maybe you will need to do something important, for me. And for Michael.

Love,
Marta

PS. If you write, send everything to the address in Zagreb, and never use my family name.

Write to: Marta c/o Sanja Paljutek.

PPS. Read the articles. They're all about our country, about Michael. About all of us.

Something strange happened to me when I finished reading Marta's letter. That's to say, nothing at all happened. I didn't feel angry, rebellious, distraught, or desperate. I didn't start shaking, feel suddenly full of hope, or fly into a rage. I felt not even a trace of panic. I felt nothing, thought nothing. It was as if a sort of surgical vacuum cleaner had emptied out my head.

And suddenly I noticed how quiet it had become around me. Even quieter than after Hugo disappeared. As if someone had turned the world's volume control to zero. Not a sound came through to me. I was thirsty; my hand reached for the bottle of Corona on the coffee table, but missed. In slow motion, the bottle tipped over, rolled soundlessly over the edge of the table, and fell to the smooth gray concrete floor. There it bounced once or twice, rolled up to the edge of the couch where I was sitting, and came to rest between my feet.

The beer foamed over the table and dripped onto the floor. Fortunately beer doesn't leave stains on concrete. I watched and waited for the drips to stop. The last drop took a long time to detach itself from the table.

When that finally happened, I nodded approvingly, stretched out on the couch, and shut my eyes. Just before I fell asleep, a thought came up, no, an image: I saw a train compartment, and Daniel Devolder sleeping opposite me.

Hey, man, what are you doing here? I managed to think, but almost instantaneously I fell into a deep sleep. Dreamless and profound.

The perfect sky is torn

If ever I fall asleep during the day—which happens fairly often, because I stay up far too late—I nearly always wake up with the feeling I've missed something. Not a great loss, you know. More as if I've drifted off in the middle of a really exciting video, and the rewind button on the remote won't work. I've missed a chunk of the film and can't pick up the thread. I'll never find out why Jerry suddenly gets on again with his ex, how Dave managed to get himself into that gorge with his Porsche, and what court case Sue is involved in now. That sort of loss. Frustrating, but not really serious, and soon forgotten.

But waking up this time was different. No hint of having missed anything.

The first thing I felt was a sense of relief. I woke up and thought, Hey, I can hear something! It was the sound of paper flapping in the breeze. Opening my eyes, I saw Marta's letter and the bundle of papers floating about on the floor: the image confirmed the sound, so I was doubly reassured. My attack of deafness must have been transitory and more than likely to do with the Mexican beer Hugo'd served me.

Next I noticed that the light had changed, the sun was low in the sky. I must have slept for hours.

Another gust of wind, and the papers flapped about like

white birds. A window banged against a wall. The thunderstorm, the forecast thunderstorm. It was really coming.

Even the weather forecasts were correct. The world was uncannily normal, and my perceptions strikingly clear. Everything was quiet and clear, in my head and around me. And that's exactly what was so strange. I should have been amazed and confused, but the only thing that confused me a bit was my lack of confusion.

That was my second thought after I woke up.

My third thought was focused on Marta's letter. With that same disconcerting clarity, I mentally scanned the lines Marta had written in her slightly awkward Dutch.

The fact that it was a red felt pen letter didn't surprise me: I had expected that. Having to call her, having to do the calling *myself*, filled me with horror—but okay, it would get done. Anna can handle this much.

Michael?

Michael's name had been mentioned. What to make of that? "Terrible things" had happened, but she was "okay now."

Was Michael okay, too? I could possibly do something important for her "and for Michael." But was he okay? Not a word about that.

And why this messing about with names and addresses, and why all this secrecy? My extensive TV experience led me to CIA, FBI, and/or Mafia business. Were they in hiding? Were they involved in illegal activities? Were they wanted? By Milosevic's henchmen or something? And what was *my* part in all this?

Finally I remembered "don't wait too long" and "call me." That needed more thinking.

My fourth thought surprised me. I thought of Daniel Devolder. A sleeping middle-aged man, with a nose that was too big and a heart problem. Where did he fit into this story? I'd thought of him just before I fell asleep. And that was weird.

The wind was getting stronger. I got up to shut the window. The crack in the glass ran right across the sky. It reminded me of something I'd seen on TV, a memorial service for the Vietnam War. The monument for the fallen in Washington was a broken mirror in the grass. So if you looked into it, you saw a cracked sky. *The perfect sky is torn.* Forever torn, something like that. What symbolism, Anna! Shaking my head, I returned to the couch, gathered the papers off the floor, pushed them into the envelope, and went to get a cloth to wipe up the remaining spilled beer, though most of it had dried up. I put the empty bottle into the recycle bin, picked up the letter, and went over to the elevator. A freight plane flew low over the warehouse, making the floor shake under my feet. At home, in Holsbeek, planes often passed over the house. Maybe that's why I had slept so deeply? Familiar sounds often make less noise than silence.

Then I got into the elevator, straining all the muscles in my arms shutting the grating, enjoying the rattling clatter I caused. Outside, it was almost windless. The sun reflected off the bare wall. Round the corner, it was windier again. A wide, busy street, lots of trucks, and beyond, the water. Across the water I saw the train station. From here, the building seemed quite small, even insignificant, but that wasn't just because of the distance. There was a ferry moored beyond, and it was taller than the station. A floating apartment building. Ostend was a seaside town, and the boats here were bigger than the houses.

And then, from its deepest entrails, the ferry emitted a blast of its horn, lower and more penetrating than the horns of all the trucks in the world. The sound ripped the bright blue sky into shreds. It rolled over the smooth surface of the water, straight at me, and hit me in the stomach, and suddenly I was overcome by fear. Instinctively, I squeezed my eyes shut and pulled my head down between my shoulders. Get under cover! flashed through my head. Get under cover! And then I knew where the fear came from: It was the war stories I had been told by my grandfather, my father's father, when I was very little. The sirens, the air-raid warnings, the shelters, the bombardments—the dull thuds as bombs struck, like earth tremors, distant at first but getting closer, like an approaching thunderstorm. Openmouthed I'd sat on his lap, listening, seeing it all happening before my eyes.

Then the ferry blasted its horn a second time, but I forced myself to keep my eyes open. The city appeared quite peaceful, nobody seemed to be concerned. No war here, the sun was shining, the air was pure and clear, not a plane in sight.

Then it sounded a third time, and the ferry slid away. It was incredible. Slowly it went, but at the same time so fast: inconceivable how such a cumbersome mass could start moving so quickly, as if a building were setting off on a trip. Mass by volume by uniform acceleration over the resistance of the water, I thought, vaguely remembering my physics exam, but of course that's not what it was about. The way that ferry slid away so irresistibly, it was as if a whole apartment building was detaching itself—complete with foundations, basements, apartments, elevators, walls, doors, windows, tables, chairs, kitchen cupboards, garbage chutes, shower curtains, wallpaper, and standard lamps on coffee tables—and breaking away from the city. The city was suffering an amputation, and it didn't even notice. Or were cities by the sea used to this?

Clouds appeared from the west. The ferry was invisible now behind other harbor buildings, and the station looked even smaller than before. As if it had been orphaned.

All the same, I had to get to the station to collect my things. I figured the distance, the best way to get there. Follow the tram tracks, then over the bridge, then along the fishing wharf with the shrimp sellers' stalls.

On the way, I thought about my grandfather, whom I'd known only briefly—he died when I was five or six—and his stories about the war, always the war. I also thought about my mother's father, whom I'd never known. Mom never said anything about her parents. What sort of stories would my Yugoslav grandad have told me if I'd known him? War stories, too, probably, but Yugoslav ones. At the time, I thought war stories were the best, they were the most exciting. Thrilling "boys' own" stories. How far was Kosovo from Zagreb, actually?

And right away my head was full of Kosovo again: NATO blunders, mutilated bodies, bombed hospitals, women in labor hit by . . . Broken glass, twisted metal. I gripped the railing of the bridge till my knuckles were white, I nearly vomited. Oh, my stupid head. Go away everything! Get out of my head.

But it wouldn't go away.

In the station, I wriggled my way quietly through the crowd, got my backpack out of the locker, threw it over my shoulder—I still had my camera bag over the other—and left through the large revolving glass door. Quite a handsome building, really. Hadn't noticed this morning. I had a brief moment of shock when I saw a pale blue sweater among the milling people, but it didn't react to my shouts. Oh, well. I don't suppose I would have reacted either. And perhaps it was someone else.

For the second time that day I started walking in the direction of my father's apartment, and slowly I could feel the thoughts of war draining out of me. I thought about tonight, the concert, Bert, what I was going to wear. Ordinary things.

I felt relieved.

I walked along the fishing wharf, past the shrimp sellers, onto the seawall. Twelve Albertina Walk, apartment 6D. The lift, the door, my key. A shower was what I wanted.

"Dad? It's me!"

He wasn't there. I checked the kitchen clock—quarter to six, plenty of time—and in the hall I stopped in front of the photo of Michael and Jonas. I traced the five-year-old tear with my finger. I hadn't done that since, well, since I tore it.

They looked good. Jonas a touch too thin, perhaps? No, not yet then. Both of them laughing their heads off. Some teeth Jonas had!

I went a step closer and looked at their eyes. They weren't looking quite straight into the lens, and that was right—yes, that was right, I suddenly remembered it—it was me they were looking at.

They were both home that day, which was unusual, because Michael was already studying in Italy, and Jonas was living in America. I was five or six. After dinner they'd wandered into the garden, and then Dad said, Stay there a second, boys, the light's just perfect. He got his Nikon and took the photo. I was standing next to him, I remember, because they were not looking at him, not into the lens (a 50mm, I'd say), but at me, their little sister. I was holding my new Barbie doll. Jonas had just given it to me, straight from America, and I was so happy I was hugging the doll like a newborn baby. That's why they'd just burst out laughing, and that's when Dad pressed the shutter button. So the fact that it was such a good photo was partly because of me. I was part of that photo, even though I wasn't in it.

And I was there, too, a week or so later, when Dad printed the photo in his improvised darkroom in the bathroom. By then my brothers had returned to their distant homes.

"And now we're going to do a really large one," he said.

"Oh, yes," I said, "so who's going to be in it?"

Watch, he said, turning the enlarger up. The smudges on the table became large and gray and blurry, but he turned a knob, and suddenly there they stood, razor sharp and almost life-size. Only Michael had white hair and Jonas had black teeth. Yuck, I said. Just wait, said Dad. He produced a thick, shiny sheet of paper out of an orange box, put that on the white base, and let the black-and-white splotches shine onto the white paper, counting five, six, seven. Then he slipped the paper into a tray of smelly piss-yellow water.

Pinch your nose and watch, he said. Breathlessly, I watched. Literally, because I had pinched my nose, and in my excitement held my mouth shut tight as well. First I saw the cherry tree appearing, leaf by leaf, light gray. Then Jonas started coming out a bit—his teeth were very white, phew—and then Michael, his hair pitch black, both smiling widely. At that very moment I thought of Italy and America, I hadn't any idea where those countries were, but felt they were terribly far away, and I still remember how much I missed my brothers at that moment. I nearly burst into tears. I think that must have been the first time I had some notion of death, of a "somewhere else" that was even farther away than just "a faraway country," because Michael and Jonas started to float in front of my eyes like angels or lost stars, apparitions or spirits from another world. Dad laughed in the dim red light, and he seemed like a magician to me.

"Weird, isn't it?" he said. "They're here, but they're not."

I nodded speechlessly. Absence and loss—what could I know about that? They looked at me and my Barbie doll and roared with laughter. Nineteen-eighty-nine. How could they know I'd tear them apart five years later?

Nineteen-ninety-nine. I was sixteen. Jonas was dead. And Michael? Ah, Michael. My finger traced the five-year-old tear. A burst of sunlight suddenly threw a bright light onto the wall and the photo. On an impulse, I got my camera and took a photo of the photo. After the click of the shutter, I paused, shaking my head.

Oh, Anna, what's happening now?

Then I picked up my bag, found the bathroom, and had a shower. Fa Body Splash, the ultimate in freshness.

With wet hair and a towel over my shoulders, I searched the fridge for a snack. I found a bowl with dried-out grains of semolina and a pot with overcooked vegetables. The failed couscous. Oh, Dad. A cracker would have to do. And a tub of strawberry yogurt. I stood by the window while I ate. More clouds were coming up in the west, and they were gray, almost black. Wouldn't be long now. I looked down.

On the seawall, far below me, the first umbrellas were going up. I hated umbrellas, but from up here they looked rather nice, like multicolored counters in a gigantic tiddlywinks game. I went back to the kitchen, dumped the yogurt container in the pale-blue rubbish bag, and suddenly saw that it was nearly eight o'clock.

Shit! Get a move on, Anna. I slipped into my jeans, hesitated a moment between a purple shirt with bat sleeves and a burgundy T-shirt, went for the shirt, raced for the door, and was sorry about the T-shirt by the time I was in the elevator. Ah, well.

There were a lot of people about on the seawall, and they were a weird lot. Hip-hoppers with duckbill caps and long shorts, post-punks with red and green mohawks, post-sixty-eighters with wraparound skirts, sandals, and clouds of patchouli wafting around them, back-to-the-seventies types in baggy pants and sideburns, guys with shaven heads and loose Adidas pants—the whole scene was there. But I also saw tourists in shorts and loud shirts, and fashionable couples—navy blazer flanked by cocktail dress, stiletto heels and lots of jewelry. And even a couple of pseuds in dinner jackets and bare feet—the latest in thing, I'd read somewhere.

I walked along with them. Occasionally I stood on tiptoes looking for a light blue sweater. In vain, of course.

After a while, I noticed that just about everybody was going the same way—my way. Most were walking fast, and there wasn't much talk. As if all of us were drawn by the same voice. As if the Pied Piper was in town. Or was it just the approaching thunderstorm? Did everybody want to get under cover before the cloudburst?

It was getting dark very rapidly now, black clouds roiling above our heads.

And then, on the horizon, just above the sea, the clouds parted like stage curtains, to reveal a blood-red sun that threw a blinding, unreal light onto the seawall. A few people stopped, exclaiming "Oooh!" as if there were fireworks, and everybody paused to watch the spectacle. It became quiet on the seawall. All the faces around me seemed to radiate a kind of orange glow. The sun often caused strange effects, especially close to the sea, my father maintained, but this really was special.

And it was over. The clouds moved together theatrically, and the sun disappeared. Thunder started rumbling softly, like cannon on a distant front. Here and there in the sky lightning flashed, far away.

People started moving again, walking toward the casino. Then the walking turned into running, soles shuffling and heels clicking on the tiles. The rain! The rain was about to come.

And just when we were nearly there, just past the bend in the seawall—that "arc of perfect grace"—it arrived. Not gradually, building up, not in a crescendo, but *wham!* instantly at full volume. The crowd surged toward the entry, toward salvation, heads down, slamming into the great glass doors, which swung open with a bang.

Only when we were inside the foyer, large as a football ground, did we stop, exhausted. Water trickled from our hair, from our clothes, making big puddles on the carpet. Behind us, on Casino Square, it was bucketing down. Taxis and limos came and went, the more expensive festival guests being escorted to the door under umbrellas. In the commotion, I suddenly spotted Hugo. He looked extremely elegant in his Armani dinner jacket, and he was chatting with a tall, thin man. The man looked at least as elegant, with his graying sideburns, his three-piece cream-colored suit, and his tanned bald head. I pushed my way toward them, but before I was halfway there, I saw the man shake Hugo's hand and disappear into the crowd. Daniel Devolder? And Hugo? What was going on?

"Hugo!"

He grinned when he saw me. "Hey, did you come on the *Titanic?*"

Yes, that's what I look like, I thought. My lovely purple shirt hung around my body like a wet flag. I returned his grin and asked, "Who was that man?"

"What man?"

"The one you were talking to. The tall thin one—"

"Yes?"

"Was that Daniel Devolder?"

"Yes . . . Why?"

Then a bell rang to announce the start of the concert.

"We're about to start," said Hugo. "Here are your tickets, F7 and F9 . . . Are you still expecting someone?"

Quickly, I looked around. The foyer was emptying. "No . . . not really."

"Go through that door. I'll see you later," said Hugo.

I looked over my shoulder once more and went in. I hadn't really expected Bert.

Mano Solo

Hugo had arranged excellent seats for me. With a bit of luck, the singer's spittle would reach this far. Might be able to see his fillings. And the little marks on the inside of his elbows. I looked around. The hall was nearly full. Strange setup, that opening concert: dead-chic hall, ankle-deep carpet, white-gloved ushers, numbered seats, plush chairs, crystal chandeliers, and glittering invited guests. All that mixing quite naturally with the drenched riffraff brazenly taking off their soaked Nikes and leaving them lying about in the aisles.

And now the beau monde was arriving, everybody who was anybody, *le tout Ostende,* as Hugo called them, and they were fashionably late so everybody could see them. Mano Solo would gladly show them his bare ass, or the back of his throat, which probably amounted to much the same thing, I thought briefly, but already the house lights were going down and the band started to play. *Le tout Ostende* indignantly tripped over their own feet and stumbled on, grumbling. I watched them, grinning, but meanwhile my eyes scanned the steeply raked seats behind me, not quite knowing who they were looking for.

Just before it was completely dark, someone sat down beside me. I hoped Bert, thought of Devolder, but it was Hugo.

"Bizarre mix," he whispered in my ear. "Bass, trombone, rhythm section and a string quartet . . . You'll see, this is going to be memorable!"

"This Devolder—" I whispered back, but suddenly the drums thundered and there he was, Mano Solo. MS.

He crept onto the stage from the wings. He was small and thin, his hair was short and curly; he wore black pants and a black, sleeveless T-shirt, and his eyes glittered behind a purple Zorro mask.

"Listen to this—" Hugo said quickly.

The singer stepped into the bright light, gripped the microphone like a weapon, and started singing. And instantly the audience was absolutely silent. As if they felt it: one final time in the spotlight, and then never again. Mano Solo sang. One moment his voice sounded very small and still, like a child watching the sun rising behind the curtain in a bedroom window; a moment later he was yelling like a despairing youth after his first night of love. Then, in turn, he sounded hoarse and weak like a patient in a cancer ward, fast like a rapper on speed, hard like a Palestinian throwing stones at Israeli soldiers, fast and murderous like a Porsche in a bend that's far too tight—but what he said and sang and shouted was always the same. It was bold and challenging, it was bitter and full of hope, and it moved every eardrum, every brain cell in the area, and every hair on my neck. He told us he was going to die, but that now he was still alive, and that we should all bloody well know this.

Know that he was still living. The audience obviously felt

he should stay that way, because a cheer went up that must have chased death far away, far beyond the horizon, like a ferry disappearing out to sea. The thousands of fans cheered him on because of that life of his, that thin silken thread. They shouted and whooped, stamped their feet and whistled on their fingers, and I didn't know what was happening to me. I gasped for breath, gripping Hugo's arm, and Hugo, too, stared at the stage, at that hardly more than one hundred pounds of flesh, that parcel of bones rattling around in a skin that was far too big, that little guy who stood there shouting as if he wanted to wrench the very soul out of that body, and the shouting sounded like life itself.

". . ." Hugo shouted something into my ear.

"What?"

". . ."

"Hell, Hugo, I can't hear you! Speak more clearly!"

His lips moved. I put my ear to his mouth.

"Living like this, dying like this!" he bellowed in my ear.

That's how it is, I thought, and meanwhile the decibels were hacking holes like craters in my middle ear—the drum, the bass, the guitars, the trombone, they hurtled and whirled through the hall, and I could feel everything trembling and shaking. The singer raged, whispered, screamed, cursed, and begged, and I could understand every single word of it, even though my French isn't all that wonderful.

He asked for silence. Four thousand throats were silent. The spotlight on him dropped out, leaving him and us in darkness. A power failure? A disappointed "Oooo" went through the audience, but he laughed briefly, with a hiccup, and reassured us.

"Doesn't matter," he said. "I look on it as a bit of a rehearsal. A preview of what's waiting for me shortly. Black, it is, and dark. And anyway, think about it for a moment—no, really, be honest. If you think about it really honestly—you love me because, well, just a bit, because I'm dying instead of you. True, isn't it?"

Then he must have given a signal, and the light came back. The string quartet started up.

"It still happens to me sometimes . . . ," he whispered into the microphone. And he was singing again:

Il m'arrive encore de temps en temps
De sortir voir s'il y a des enfants
Il m'arrive encore des mariages soudains
Frôlés dans la rue, le temps d'un parfum
Il m'arrive encore de leur faire l'amour
De mentir un instant
Il m'arrive encore de pleurer sur mon sort
D'avoir peur de la mort
Mais je suis vivant!

I still go out at times
To see if there are children about
It still happens to me—a whiff of perfume, a passing touch
In the street—and I imagine a sudden wedding
It still happens to me—making love to them

I still pretend to myself, for just a moment
I still cry over my fate
I still fear death
But I am alive!

At this last shout the audience nearly exploded, and inside me something exploded, too. I clapped my hands over my ears and screamed along with the crowd. Nobody heard me, but my scream was different, it came from somewhere else. My scream was five years old, and no one knew where it came from. Hugo did. Hugo saw it. Hugo saw me and heard me. He put his arm around my shoulder and squeezed me against him, but I tore myself away.

I ran from the hall, through the corridors and the foyer, through the glass doors. Outside. There, in the fresh air, on Casino Square, I stood gasping for breath, my face wet with tears, and screamed. With my eyes closed, I threw my head back and screamed again. My scream echoed around the wet buildings. Nobody had run after me. Nobody had heard me. Luckily. Behind the dark balcony doors of the apartment buildings everything remained quiet and dark.

What a soap, Anna! Summary in *TV Week*: "*Anna (16) appears to be a carefree teenager. But suddenly she's confronted with a great sorrow from her past. During a concert she experiences a violent crisis, but once she has come through that, she is ready for new challenges, a new life . . .*"

Well, you all know what you can do with it, ladies and gentlemen, dear viewers: sometimes the cliché is more real than life itself! Was it my fault that my whole life was nothing but one great cliché?

The square was empty and dark, still shiny from the rain. Right at its center stood a gigantic stone hand, a symbol of . . . a monument for . . . couldn't quite think of it, though my father had told me. I took a deep breath and walked over to it. I sat down in its large palm. The rough stone felt cool against my back. Bit damp, but I didn't mind that. I sat down and tried to think.

I'd overestimated what I could do, I realized. Thought I could handle it all. That I would be well equipped after two letters like that, and after my heroic journey to the seaside. Watch out, world, here comes the new Anna! Ah, bullshit! Anna was a coward, always would be. She cringed in fear at the slightest noise, like a scared rabbit. Anna was just a little girl. Anna just wanted to be an ordinary little girl. You know, ordinary, just a girl. An ordinary girl . . .

My new life

When my big brother Jonas died of AIDS, I was a celebrity at school for a while. I was nearly eleven, in fifth grade, and AIDS was trendy. We were swamped with information campaigns by the government and free condoms from progressive magazines. During recesses, my girlfriends huddled together in the playground, giggling, telling excited tales of sex and boys and condoms. I stood at the edge of the circle, shrugging.

"Hah, you don't even know what you're talking about."

"Oh, no? And you reckon you do?"

"I do, actually. I just happen to have a brother who's died of AIDS."

And they swirled around me. "Really? Truly? AIDS? Gee! Tell us, Anna!"

And I told them. And I enjoyed it. I enjoyed it so much that the principal became seriously concerned and informed my parents. But at that time my parents were unreachable, because Dad was too busy with his own sorrow, and Mom was away traveling. I was staying at my uncle Paul's for a few months. And Uncle Paul, who was a doctor, told the principal it would be best to let me be, that it was part of my grieving and so on (stage one of the process), and so the principal let me be. It would pass. And I told more stories, gave an incredibly cool talk to a totally silent class (A–, pat on the back from teacher, the whole class sniffling), enjoyed it for a little longer, and then it was suddenly over. I clammed up. Stage two of the process, the closing-up stage, said Uncle Paul (ha, ha!), and that was actually good timing, because just about then AIDS was no longer trendy. So, just before they would have started complaining, "Not her again, with her AIDS and her dead brother," I had conveniently clammed up. Not another word out of me. The principal breathed a sigh of relief, and my reputation improved even more. When I moved to high school (a year early, but I absolutely insisted on changing schools, and I was bright enough), my reputation preceded me. The principal and teachers handled me with kid gloves because I was the girl-who-had-been-through-so-much, and the other students in my class looked up with admiration, but a bit nervously, to that girl-with-a-dead-brother. Mind what you say to her, she has a sharp tongue. As I said, I trailed a reputation.

Meanwhile, my parents had come home. For the moment they had finished grieving and traveling, and the three of us settled back at Holsbeek. Not the four of us, no, my other big brother Michael went on commuting between Italy and Sarajevo for a while. So my parents found me right in the middle of my stage two (the clamming-up stage, that is) and thought it would be wise to get me into therapy to the tune of two sessions and a heap of money every week. But that didn't do much good, because two years later, when Michael disappeared without a trace in that bloody country of his, that country without a name, I didn't say a word about him. I had learned my lesson.

I became the girl-with-those-two-dead-brothers. They still had to treat me cautiously, because I still had a sharp tongue. Around that time, my hormones became active, and boys just about queued up for me. I could choose, catch, and dump whoever I wanted, but I only fell in love when I really wanted to myself. *Never,* in other words. I drove teachers to exasperation, parents to grief, and classmates to muttered admiration. Except for the boys I dumped. I simply drove them to despair. One of them nearly jumped out of a window because of me, number eleven or twelve, Dieter was his name. He lived on the sixteenth floor. That actually gave me a fright.

"Elle habite au vingtième ça fait treize étages plus haut que le septième ciel . . ." I caught myself singing something from Mano Solo: "She lives on the twentieth floor, that's thirteen floors up from seventh heaven . . ." Well, singing . . .

"Anna!"

What now? I knew that voice, but it sounded strange. Hollow and muffled.

"Annaaa!"

He knew me, obviously, but didn't seem to like me. He shouted my name like an obscenity. Oh, no, not . . .

"Bert?"

"Anna! You slut!"

Just what I needed. I knew straightaway what the matter was. Bert hardly ever drank, but when he did . . .

Slowly, I walked up to him, until I could see his eyes. They looked wild and glassy.

"You're a slut, Anna! How is it going with Hugo, Anna?"

"No, Bert, no!"

"Ha! Hugo! I knew it as soon as you . . ."

God, he was drunk!

"Of course, Hugo! I know you and Hugo are . . . Oh, oh, oh, Anna, oh, oh, oh, mind you, I can understand it. If I was a woman, I might go for Hugo myself . . ."

"Bert!" I was getting really angry now.

"Oh, oh, is Miss Anna angry? I am so sorry! Have I said something I shouldn't? Have I been rude? Oh, Miss Anna, please forgive poor slobby Bert. You know, he doesn't understand what real life's like, he's far too coarse for that. Of course, there are more important things in life. . . . Because Hugo means success, doesn't he? Hugo offers much better prospects than some besotted pimply teenager like Bert, who'll never become more than a mechanic or something—"

"Bert, please, stop it!" My voice stuck in my throat.

"—and ab-so-lute-ly hasn't studied enough to understand Miss Anna's problems. . . . Because Miss Anna's problems . . . Oh, Bertie, they're way beyond your shallow little brain! Otherwise, Miss Anna would have explained things to you long ago . . . for instance why she keeps on coming after you and then dumping you like a piece of shit. Wouldn't she, Bert?"

I was horrified. I could barely recognize his voice. Normally, Bert had a pleasing voice. He could even sing, a bit like that guy in Simply Red. Now his croaking voice echoed hideously over Casino Square, and I felt only pity and disgust. I couldn't help him, not at that moment. I gestured helplessly, turned, and ran away.

Gutless? Perhaps. Bert thought so. He sneered, and it cut through my soul.

"Yes, run away! That's the only thing you're good at!"

And I ran away. Faster and faster I ran, along the seawall, over the wet, gleaming tiles, and I heard his stumbling steps behind me. Every now and then he shouted something, but I couldn't hear what. After a while, I could hear nothing but my own gasping breath. The seawall was deserted, and the only thing I could think of was to get home. Home, that was my father's place. I stormed into the hall, couldn't find the light switch, couldn't remember where I'd put my key, and was digging around feverishly in my bag when the glass entrance doors were hurled open with a bang.

"Anna!"

"Bert! No!"

He came at me threateningly till he stood just in front of me, swaying and breathing heavily, his eyes rolling. I ducked. Then he suddenly stood still, a shudder went right through his body, he gagged once or twice and started to vomit uncontrollably. It just gushed out of him. He slid down and slumped crookedly against the wall. A sour stench spread through the hall.

Oh, no. This is your new life, Anna. Ready for new challenges?

Briefly, I stood staring at Bert, my hand clasped over my mouth—do something, Anna, do something! I knelt down and tugged at his shoulders. His head flopped around as if it would fall off his body any minute, and a thin stream of milk-white spit ran from the corner of his mouth. I got a tissue and wiped his mouth clean, stupidly said his name a few times, and then I gave up. What now? Get a doctor? Perhaps I could ring from my dad's apartment, but then I would have to leave Bert here by himself. . . .

"Can I help?"

I turned round abruptly and looked into the eyes of Daniel Devolder. He frowned.

"Anna! What are you doing here?"

"And you?"

"I live here, remember?"

Of course. Dumb question.

"Shall we take care of this young man first?" He bent over the unconscious Bert, lifted one of his eyelids, felt his pulse. "Has he been drinking?"

I nodded.

"A lot?"

"I don't know. He hardly ever drinks. I wasn't there, he just followed me after the concert—"

"Tell me about it later. Come on, give me a hand." He grabbed hold of Bert under one arm, hoisted him up, and slung him over his shoulder. "You take the other arm."

Bert groaned softly. He was as heavy as a bag of wet sand, but we managed to get to the elevator.

"Four," panted Devolder. "Press number four." Two floors below Dad.

"Mind your heart," I said.

"Keep quiet, will you."

The elevator was so small that it was pretty easy to keep Bert upright between us and the walls. His light blue sweater was covered in dark blue spots. I noticed that his shoelaces were undone.

On the landing, Devolder got out his key and, with difficulty, pushed the door half open.

"The hall is still full of cardboard boxes. First door on the right, there's a bed there."

Falling and stumbling, we managed to get Bert onto the bed. He sighed heavily, swallowed with difficulty, and made little gurgling sounds through his open mouth. Like a goldfish, only with his eyes closed. Devolder got his black bag, lifted Bert's eyelid, shone a little flashlight into his eye, and felt his throat.

"What's wrong with him?" I asked.

"Probably an allergic reaction. Did you say he never drinks?"

"Almost never."

Bert's throat was now covered in red spots. Devolder got out a stethoscope.

"Anything I can do?" I said.

"The bathroom is to the right, at the end of the passage. Go and get something to freshen him up a bit."

Bathroom? Freshen up? End of the passage. I found the light

switch. Freshen up, freshen up . . . Ah, here, yes, that'll do. I held a towel under the tap and ran back to the bedroom. Water dripped onto the linoleum. Bert was now breathing more quietly, I thought. Devolder looked at the dripping towel.

"Perfect," he said.

"Have you given him something?"

He shook his head. "Sleep," he said. "That's all this boy needs. Take his sweater off and clean him up a bit, could you?"

I felt like a nurse in a hospital series. Something useful. He lifted Bert's shoulders, and I pulled the sweater over Bert's lolling head. Then I patted his hot forehead with the wet, cool towel, smoothed his hair, and wiped his face, throat, chest, and arms clean. His hands, his fingers. I pulled his shoes off and put them under the bed.

"When you've finished, pull a blanket over him."

"Certainly, Doctor."

Devolder gave a brief smile and left the room. Still playing my nurse's part, I pulled Bert's dirty jeans off, allowed my eyes to glide all over him for a moment, sighed, and put a blanket over him. Planted a quick kiss on his forehead. "Sorry, man," I said.

Bert groaned softly in his sleep. I wondered what he was dreaming.

I switched off the light and left the door ajar. At the end of the passage I saw light.

"Anna?" Devolder called.

I stood in the doorway. He was sitting in an armchair by the window.

"Would you like a drink?" he said. Two glasses already stood before him.

"Oh, yes, please," I said.

Without asking what I would like, he poured white wine for me, too. A dark green bottle with an Italian label.

"Sit down."

The living room was bare, and empty of cartons. By the window was an antique desk with a mahogany chair. An off-white couch stood against the wall, with a standard lamp next to it. Then stacks of books, and on the marble mantelpiece a row of CDs and, strangely, a boom box. Dozens of photographs stood leaning against the wall, mostly black-and-white, mounted in plain frames. I recognized Bill Brandt, William Klein, Mary Ellen Marks, Manuel Alvárez Bravo, and Henri Cartier-Bresson. Original prints, by the looks of them. I whistled through my teeth.

"Beautiful photos you've got there."

"Expensive, you mean." I nodded and drank. The wine was delicious and instantly went to my head. Just like Hugo's beer, this afternoon.

"Doctors are supposed to make lots of money, aren't they?"

"I like spending my money on lovely things."

I took a long, steady look at him. I still found it hard to see him as a doctor.

"Are you sure Bert's—?"

"Don't worry. He'll sleep now for a long time, and very deeply, and tomorrow he'll wake up with a whopping headache and swear he'll never touch another drop of alcohol."

Or me, I thought.

"It's my fault," I said.

"What is?"

"That he's been drinking. I've been really awful to him, today."

"Listen, your private lives—"

I shook my head. "No, no, please. I'm really grateful you helped him. And me. I really don't expect you to get involved in our personal—" I interrupted myself. What was it I'd been going to ask him?

"Would you like some cheese? I've got some Leerdam, I think."

"Nice," I said. "I haven't had all that much to eat today."

"Leerdam goes well with Italian wine."

He pushed his chair back and went to the kitchen. Then I remembered what I'd been going to ask.

"Oh, yes . . . Were you a GP, or—?"

"What did you say?" he called from the kitchen.

"When you were a doctor, did you specialize in anything?"

"Tropical medicine," he called back.

I suddenly felt uncomfortable again, like this morning in the train, when he looked at me in that way as if he knew me from somewhere. And slowly I started to realize. Tropical medicine, the disease from Africa, *the* disease . . .

"There's only one Institute for Tropical Medicine in Belgium," I said hesitantly, getting up and going over to the kitchen.

"That's right," he said. His apartment had an open

kitchen, separated from the living room by a counter. I leaned on it with my elbows, like in a café. He was cutting a piece of cheese into cubes.

". . . the disease of the nineties, *the* disease . . ." My words stumbled over themselves, like my thoughts.

"Antwerp," he helped. He didn't look up but smiled, his eyebrows raised.

We'd got there. I swallowed, was silent for a moment, didn't want to ask anything, and then asked it anyway.

"Did you know Jonas? Jonas Bracke?"

"No need to be so worried."

"Did you know him?"

He breathed deeply through his big nose and nodded. "I saw you there, too—that final week."

"In Wilrijk? In the University Hospital?"

Jonas. Sixty-five pounds. Tube in his nose. Stifling room with too many people. Mom cut his fingernails.

"He was my patient."

So I was right. That's where I'd seen him. And he me. Room 212. There was laughter. There had never been so much laughter in a hospital as in room 212. Certainly not in this department. Jonas was forever joking. He wore those hospital pajamas with short sleeves. His arms were nearly transparent, I could count his veins. His hair was as thin as an old man's.

"Did he joke with you, Dr. Devolder?"

"Daniel."

"What?"

"Just call me Daniel, please!" He sounded mildly irritated. "All that 'doctor' business makes me nervous."

"Why?"

"Makes me feel so—"

"Doctorish?"

"Yes."

"So what did Jonas call you?"

"He called me Doc, like the fat dwarf in *Snow White*. He thought it was a good name for a doctor. Stuttering and scared."

"But with a big heart, I suppose?"

He raised his eyebrows, holding his head at an angle, as if he was thinking about it.

"Almost all of them were like him," he said thoughtfully, and turned back to the cheese board.

"Who?"

"My patients. The guys with AIDS. The ones that were seropositive. Of course there were a few bastards among them, and perverts and egoists and spoiled crybabies. But most of them were like him, like Jonas. Young and strong—well, strong—they had lived freely and intensely, and generally knew more about living than we, their doctors, did. We were in awe. How did Hugo describe it? 'Like a surfer riding the waves.'"

"Hey, you know Hugo, too?"

I was curious how he would react. It really was him I'd seen chatting with Hugo before the concert.

"Of course I know Hugo. He was there, in the hospital. And John and Amy I met, too."

"John is dead."

"Oh?"

"Last year, heart attack. Mom went to the funeral."

"In New York?"

"Long Island."

"Great guy, John. I only met him once, but I knew right away. . . ." He closed his eyes, as if he were trying to recall the scene. "Jonas's room was always crowded, I remember it well. So many friends. There were those people from Amsterdam, his fellow students from Louvain, and Paul and Amos, his New York buddies, and—"

"—Michael?"

He hesitated at this. "Michael, too, yes."

I didn't reply immediately. "Are you still in touch with those people?"

"Only Hugo. He always sends me a postcard when he's abroad. And we ring each other occasionally."

"What for?"

He raised his eyebrows. "To talk," he said softly. "To talk, like you and I are doing now." I stared at him, a bit taken aback. But he turned around, took a jar of mustard from the fridge, put some in a bowl, and placed it on the cheese board.

"Some cheese?" he asked. I shook my head.

"Um, Doc," I said, "you must know about Michael, then?"

"Yes."

Now we were both silent for a while.

"Come on, let's go and sit down," he said then. We went back to the living room and he put the cheese board down on the floor between us. I thought urgently. Talk, he'd said. A conversation. Where was I going to start?

"This morning, on the train," I asked, "did you recognize me right away?"

"Not right away. But when you said your name was Anna, well . . ."

"The card you gave me . . ."

"What's the matter with that?"

"It gave me a shock."

"Oh, why's that?"

"My father lives here, too. Did you know that?"

He opened his eyes wide. "No!" he said.

"Six D," I said.

"No!" he said once more, and I concluded from his reaction that coincidences really do happen.

He asked how my parents were, and I told him about their problems, how they did their best, not always too successfully. When I said something about my fear of the past, and how my parents always kept silent about it, he suddenly got up and said, "I've got something to show you." He rummaged among the stacks of books, and handed me a very thin little volume. It was a book of New York photos, showing all sorts of New Yorkers, ordinary people, posed stylishly in their natural environment, shot in sharp, clear black-and-white, looking candidly and unself-consciously into the lens. There was a bowling alley manager from Brooklyn, a tobacconist from Queens, a Manhattan taxi driver, and a musical instrument restorer from Staten Island. My eyes filled with tears as

I leafed through the book, because I thought of Jonas, who had lived there and who could have met these people in the street, on his way to work, greeting them with his broad smile: "Hi, Joe," and "Hi, Bill," and "Hi, Veronica." Then Devolder said, "Have a look at the fly leaf," so I went back and read the inscription: *To my friend Doc Devolder etcetera.* I recognized Jonas's wobbly handwriting, and I howled like a small child, tears pouring from my eyes.

Devolder jumped up and was about to head for the kitchen, but I shook my head and stopped him.

"No tissues, Doc, no tissues. Please tell me about Jonas." I wiped away the snot and all the tears with my sleeve. "Tell me about Jonas."

And that's what Devolder did. For hours he talked to me about Jonas, and I told him about my countless boyfriends, about my travel phobia, and about my great sorrow as the girl-with-the-dead-big-brother. I even told him about the torn photo, and how upset I was about that. He nodded when I told him that.

"I suspected something like that this morning in the train, when we were talking about those photos."

"Really?" I said, and started crying all over again. Devolder poured me another glass of wine.

"And your other big brother?" he said then, and I told him about Michael, who absolutely had to go and save the world, and about Mom's grief, which she finally seemed to have come to terms with, and then Devolder said, "Michael was a very special person."

And I bit my lip, looked at him, wondering if I should tell him, and told him anyway. Everything. About Hugo's letter (red felt pen, I said, careful, Doc, don't mention anything to Holsbeek!) and about Marta's letter, and that I had absolutely no idea what to do next, couldn't he help me, give me some good advice or something, please, Doc? He looked at me for rather a long time, I thought, but that could just be my imagination. Then he asked if he could have a look at Marta's letter; he was particularly interested in the articles, he said. "Of course," I said, but realized the envelope was in my camera bag, and my camera bag was at Dad's, at number 6D, and I really didn't dare turn up there at this hour. "What's the time, actually, Doc?"

"Bedtime," he said, pushing back his chair.

Dizzy from too much white wine and from way too much past, I crawled into bed with Bert. Into that strange, narrow bed. Bert was still very sound asleep, and I didn't wake him up, oh no, but I got undressed and cuddled up close to him. Every now and then he snored a bit, and his breath stank, but I didn't think it was too awful.

I was tired, so tired, and the last thing I heard was the sound of the surf. Tourists by the seaside often complain they can't sleep because of the roar of the surf, but then, most tourists are off their heads.

and what about Michael?

Way past Bruges

I don't remember much about the trip home. All sorts of things went wrong: several hours' delay (a power cable had been damaged in yesterday's thunderstorm), two pushy Canadians who kept rambling on about Leonard Cohen, and a lost ticket. Normally I would have been worried stiff, but now none of it seemed to bother me.

That was due to my hangover. Till way past Bruges there was such a hullabaloo underneath my skull, it nearly felt like a high. As if someone had popped my head in the microwave. On high. Heating occurs automatically through the friction of the molecules. Chemistry exam. I was never going to drink white wine again.

Occasionally, red and yellow spots appeared before my eyes and I hardly knew where I was, and if I shut my eyes I saw flashes of yesterday. Film images, with me in the leading role. I thought Anna wasn't bad, for a first-time actress.

Uncomfortable at first, on the platform at Louvain, but very soon more assured and improvising brilliantly in her confrontation with the perfect stranger, Devolder. About the scene with Bert on the wharf with the fishing boats I had no opinion, that still hurt too much. The meeting with my father was a bit of a failure—I figured that was partly his fault. He hadn't been responsive enough. The outburst of fury in the loft I thought was exceptionally well done. And then Marta's letter, my two brothers' photo, Mano Solo, Devolder's flat . . . It was all a bit mixed up, there were gaps in the continuity, and the editing wasn't really right, but Anna hadn't done a bad job, I thought. You could see her grow into the part. A new Anna was born.

And then I decided the name Anna no longer suited me. From now on, I wanted to be officially known as Ann, as my best friends already called me. Out with Anna. I had always hated that name.

The thundering in my head gave way to a thin whistling. I started seeing lights, I floated farther and farther away, and all sound died away. Even the two Canadians finally shut up—they probably suspected me of using quantities of mind-expanding substances—so it became really still around me.

White wine is an excellent mind-expanding substance, especially if used under medical supervision.

Hours later, when I got off the train at Louvain, I was back to normal. I was tired and hungry, my clothes were sticking to my body, my luggage was as heavy as lead, but my head was washed clean, like the sky after a thunderstorm. I knew exactly what I had to do.

First I'd ring Dad, to reassure him. Tell him I'd gotten home safely and all that.

Then Devolder, to say thank you. And to apologize for having left this morning without saying a word. And to ask him how Bert was, too.

Then Hugo? No, Hugo was for later.

Zagreb. Next I would ring Zagreb. Marta. (Sigh!)

In that order.

Okay, Anna. Ann.

And I'd have to be careful, of course, because my mother was not to know anything. Let's see, today was Sunday (it was, wasn't it? yes), so I could do the whole lot tomorrow while she was at work. Should be okay. Good. And where did that bus to Holsbeek leave? Ah, over there. Laboriously I edged my way past the excavations and barriers and fences of the Louvain Station Square, and I managed. I managed.

In Holsbeek, the house was empty and silent. Where could she be? Of course, she hadn't expected me so early, but still . . . Ah well, I could start on my plan right away.

So, first to ring Dad. I dumped my backpack in the hall and went to the phone. Answering machine. I hated answering machines, even more than phones. No, no message.

I peeled off a yellow Post-It and scribbled, "Ring Dad." One down.

Now for Devolder. His card was in the pocket of my jeans, I remembered. I keyed in his number. Engaged. I tapped on the card with my fingernail and put it back in my pocket.

Now for that number in Zagreb. Marta's friend, what was her name again? Sanja something. I got Marta's envelope out of my backpack and picked up the phone. I took a deep breath. Here we go.

00-385-

No, better use the phone in the living room, I could sit down comfortably there. Hello, chair by the phone. Hello, vase without flowers. I'd been away all of one day, and already the house looked different. I kicked my Nikes into a corner and took my socks off.

00-385-

Suddenly, I was incredibly thirsty. My throat felt full of sand. That white wine, oh dear. My voice would sound really awful, and after all those years . . . No good. So, get a drink.

I put the receiver down, went to the kitchen, and opened the fridge. There was fruit juice, wrong brand, but I was thirsty. I poured a glass, downed it in one gulp, poured another glass, and took it over to the phone. I drank some more and put the half-empty glass on the coffee table. Oops, spilled some. Get the dishcloth right away, Anna, or it will leave a nasty mark on the wood. I went to the kitchen, held the dishcloth under the tap, and so on and so on . . .

Get the picture?

I didn't even get close to ringing.

00-385- Shit!

I grabbed a Post-It and scrawled "Ring Marta." I crumpled it up, went to the kitchen, put it in the wrong recycle bin, and walked into the garden.

The grass was still wet, I could feel it between my bare toes. The table stood under the cherry tree, but it wasn't set. Small puddles lay in the depressions in the wood. Memories of rain. I tipped the table on its side, let the water run away between the boards, and went to get a towel. With unusual energy, I wiped the table. Then I wiped dry a chair, sat down, and shut my eyes. My headache was still there, I suddenly noticed. I went to find some aspirin in the medicine cabinet in the bathroom. Only two left. I dropped them in a glass and filled it with water. I watched while they dissolved, bubbling and hissing, until they were quite gone. I poured the stuff down my throat, swallowing with difficulty. It left a filthy taste in my mouth, so back to the kitchen for more fruit juice. I emptied the carton into a clean glass, went to sit by the phone again, and keyed in a number.

"Hello, Hugo?" Yes, Hugo after all. But his cell phone was on voice mail. I keyed in another number.

Now Dad's line was busy.

Another one.

Devolder wasn't answering the phone.

I gave up.

I went back to the garden. The deck chair was pretty dry. I lowered the back a few notches and lay down. It was slightly cloudy, a bit sultry. Summer was definitely here. I shut my eyes and tried to think about something else, but failed. My headache was getting worse.

Where was my mother? That was something I thought about.

If she wasn't there on a Sunday, there had to be something going on, and that had to be something to do with Hugo's letter. She wasn't blind, my mother, and she had been perfectly aware that there was something very special about that letter.

Would she have gone off again? To see her Croatian contacts? I knew there was someone in Brussels. Or had she perhaps even gone behind my back to talk to Hugo? No, impossible . . . Hugo would never . . . Red felt pen, remember? And yet . . . If she had confronted him . . .

And Dad. How much would Dad know? Nothing from me, obviously. But Mom would surely have told him about the letter. Perhaps not. Perhaps she'd wanted to spare him, the way I'd wanted to spare her. The way I wanted to spare both of them.

Terrific. Red felt pens all round, hallelujah, we were all back to square one.

And slowly, slowly, it began to dawn on me that I hadn't done all that well either, down there by the beach.

Did you, Anna? Ann?

Yes, I hear you, damn you! Don't shout like that, I've got a headache!

I made my thoughts as small and quiet as I could, but they sounded loud and clear in my aching head. I shut my eyes, but then images came, and more images. A whole new movie in my head, but a very different one this time.

I saw myself running away, through the glass doors of the casino. Gasping for breath, I stood in that great square, still shiny with rain. I was running away from Mano Solo, yes, from the whole AIDS-life-and-death scene, and from my big brother Jonas. I was running away from all that. I couldn't take it anymore. But admit it, Anna: more than anything you were running away from Hugo, weren't you? Admit it, Anna!

Hugo, who knew more about Michael? Hugo, who didn't even want to know what Marta had written? Why didn't Hugo want to know? Was he afraid of something? Or did he really know more? Why didn't he even so much as ask you what Marta had written? You should have had at least one try, Anna, to find out something from him. Once, at least once, you should have asked him. In the loft, when he had made himself scarce so suddenly . . . But you did nothing, Anna, nothing, you didn't even ask him. You just ran away!

And early this morning, Anna, didn't you run away as well? You did, didn't you?

I saw myself clambering out of the narrow bed, in Devolder's flat. It was still very early and quiet. Except in my head, which was full of roaring and banging like a building site, but I got up all the same. Bert was still fast asleep next to me. I dressed in a great hurry and crept out. I took the lift to 6D—there, too, all was quiet—grabbed my backpack and my camera bag. I saw myself run down the wharf like a thief caught in the act, to the station, to the station . . .

You were dizzy with sleep and feeling horribly sick, Anna, admit it, but you wanted to get away, just away, away, away! Home. Without seeing anyone, without a word, because that was easiest. Away from here. Away from everything. Bert, Devolder, Dad, Hugo . . . Jonas, Michael . . . Oh, Anna!

Things really weren't going well in my head. I sank back into my deck chair, opened and closed my eyes, but it didn't help.

And Michael? I thought, over and over again. And what

about Michael? That's why you bloody well traveled to Ostend in the first place, Anna, didn't you? And what about Michael now?

How are things with Michael now?

Nothing, I knew absolutely nothing about Michael.

When Mom came home—around six, I guess, the sun had just disappeared behind the big apartment block I had finally managed to think about something else.

"Hey," she said. "You're here already?"

"No," I said.

"Did you have a good time?" She didn't say where she had been, and I didn't ask.

"Terrific," I said, my eyes closed. Silence.

"Take a lot of photos?"

"Not a single one," I lied. (I swallowed. A photo of a photo, that didn't count. That wasn't really a photo, was it?)

"Oh," she said, and then asked, "Did you see Bert?"

"Yes, why?"

"No reason."

I opened one eye. She looked tired, and she noticed me noticing. She tried to smile, but couldn't manage.

"How's Dad? Did you ring him today?"

"Mm. No. Okay, I think. Why?"

She bit her lip, looking at me sideways. "Are you hungry? I could order a pizza—"

I sat up straight, frowning, as if I wanted to ask her something really serious.

"Mom, tell me, what do you think—"

"Yes?" she said hopefully.

"Should I wear my Levi's tomorrow, or that new skirt from Delia's?"

"Tomorrow?"

"Hello? End-of-year party? At school?"

She looked at me, wide-eyed. A sigh. Oh, that. Then she said, "Sure you don't want a pizza?"

I slumped back in my deck chair. No, I said, curtly, I really wasn't hungry.

Really, I added more gently, I didn't need anything. Nothing, really, Mom, don't go to any trouble.

I could have cried.

I really didn't need anything. No mother, no father, no dead brother, no two dead brothers, no boyfriend, no friend of my brothers, nothing.

And definitely no pizza.

The next few days

The next few days nothing happened.

Oh, except on Monday, of course, June 21, graduation day at school. A mass in the stifling school chapel that went on far too long, a speech by the principal behind a squealing microphone that went on far too long ("You are the future, the road ahead is wide open before you, grasp it with both hands," and more colorful language like that), and then far too much cheap bubbly and far too much lukewarm, dubious fruit juice in plastic cups, and endless bowls of limp paprika crisps and stale nuts.

Dad was there too (I'd finally got him on the phone that morning, No, no, he hadn't been worried at all, what gave me that idea, and yes, he was getting into the car right away). He hugged me and congratulated me, and was really pleased, I think, but before I could get him by himself, he had to leave.

"Hey, Dad, I wanted to ask you—"

"Not now, I've got to rush. Bye, Irina, I'll call you—"

Mom nodded absently. She was deep in conversation with my biology teacher, maybe she had a bit of a crush on the guy, but she seemed to be rather too casual with Dad. Or did I just think so?

Whatever, I thought, let them sort it out.

Bert was leaning against a table in a corner of the hall, tearing beer mats into strips. I went over.

"Hangover?"

"You bet." He grinned without looking at me. A waiter came past with nothing but champagne on his tray, and despite all yesterday's solemn oaths I took two glasses from the tray and pressed one into Bert's hand.

"Cheers."

"Cheers, Ann."

Too much alcohol is bad at our age, my mother says, and I think she's probably right, but that evening Bert and I finished up snuggled together in one bed, and it was even narrower than the bed at Devolder's.

But the next morning I took a sheet of paper (unlined, 20 pound bond) and wrote:

Dear Bert,

There's no point talking, I think. Talking would hurt too much. But I always think talking is going to hurt too much . . .

I crumpled the paper into a ball and flung it into the wastepaper basket. I took a fresh sheet and wrote:

Dear Bert,

Last night was wonderful, and I'll keep this memory for the rest of my life. I like you, I really do, but . . .

I crumpled the paper into a ball etcetera. I broke into a sweat. How is it possible, Ann, how in God's name is it possible? For the first time in my life I couldn't bear the thought of someone hurting because of me. I wanted to do something about it, I wanted to bloody do something about it, but I didn't know how. How could I? Nobody had ever taught me how.

I went downstairs, and once again dragged a deck chair into the garden, stretched out, and checked the apartment block on Fontein Street. All curtains were closed, nobody home. I took my bikini top off, and then the bottom. Get lost, the lot of you.

The phone rang, and I waited till it switched to the answering machine. I heard Bert's voice, but couldn't understand what he said. Almost immediately, I fell asleep.

A couple of hours later, I went inside, yawning. I saw three flashes on the answering machine. Three messages, probably Bert three times. I pressed delete, and went off to the bathroom to look for sunscreen. My mother didn't come home. I cooked some pasta, stirred a can of tuna into it, and ate that in front of the TV. Diet Coke. Channel surfing till midnight. Very bad night's sleep because of the heat and my sunburned skin. And because of everything going on in my head.

Cerebral cortex. A headache occurs when the cerebral cortex is pressed too close to the skull. Or something. (I'd failed biology.)

And the next few days nothing really happened.

Mom usually came home very late and appeared at breakfast with bags under her eyes, muttering something about a meeting that had gone on and on, and a café afterward. And hurried off to work. Bye, Mom. I waited for the sound of the front door slamming and the hum of her Ford Fiesta. The house to myself. I squashed bananas in a bowl, added muesli and low-fat yogurt, and sat in the garden. The barometer kept floating above I don't know how many pounds per square inch, and I sweated like a pig. Occasionally, when I wasn't too tired, I went down two blocks to rent a video from Video King. *Rear Window, Manhattan, Sleepless in Seattle, Strangers on a Train, It Could Happen to You, Casablanca, Four Weddings and a Funeral, The English Patient, L'Amant, Armageddon.* Unforgettable moments.

Once I watched twenty episodes of *Friends*, till three o'clock in the morning. Afterward, I felt as if I'd eaten ten bags of chips: your hunger is gone, but you haven't really eaten, and all that's left is a sick feeling in your stomach.

Every now and then, I sat by the phone and tried to dial a number. It never worked. Oh yes, once: I got Kristel and frightened myself to death. Accidentally dialed her number. She talked forever about her grandmother's funeral (on the day of the graduation party, that's why I hadn't seen her there), about her stupid family, aunts with wet kisses and cretinous nephews, about the new clothes shop in the main street and about her new boyfriend, who knew the first 107 episodes of *Star Trek* by heart. No, really, Ann, I swear, he knows every little bit of dialogue, a real weirdo, a real . . . what do you call them, real *Star Trek* fans? We tried to think of the word, with a lot of giggling, the way you're supposed to, but we couldn't remember. She was one boyfriend up on me now, I remarked absently. Oh, really? she said, she'd lost count, and we should urgently make plans.

Yes, absolutely, I said, sure. See you soon, Kristel. See you soon, Ann.

"Trekkies," I said aloud as I hung up. That's what you call *Star Trek* fanatics.

And then I tried to dial that other number again.

00-385-

I slammed the receiver down. No go.

Cynically, I congratulated myself. Well done, Anna/Ann! Apart from your travel phobia, your phobia about the past, and your people phobia, you've now developed phone phobia! Well done, girl, keep it up!

I went into the bathroom, carefully applied sunscreen all over, and stretched out in my deck chair. I'd probably get skin cancer at forty, but meanwhile, I was getting a nice tan.

Every night, I tossed and turned until my sheets were tangled in a knot. Once, I heard the phone ring in the middle of the night. The answering machine kicked in, but Mom ran down the stairs and picked up. My eyes wide open in the dark, I overheard a conversation in Serbo-Croatian. I can understand a little Serbo-Croatian, but Mom was talking so fast all I could make out were the words: "Marta," "Markovic," "nothing," "letter," and "till tomorrow."

It was now halfway through July, and during the last week I had thought less and less of my weekend by the sea. And if I ever did give it a thought, it seemed like a dream. As if I hadn't really experienced it. Like a film in which I hadn't even played a part, just seen on TV. Saw a really interesting *National Geographic* documentary last night about the state of the bird population in the Persian Gulf. So beautifully filmed, it was as if I was really there. I could almost feel the tar on my wings. Is this real, Ann? Pinch your arm.

Meanwhile, the Sunset Festival was finished. Hugo was probably back at work in Brussels.

Dad, I supposed, would be busy too, with his casino project.

Mom was back at her translation bureau.

Bert? Oh, Bert . . .

And Devolder, what would he be up to now?

And right then, the phone rang. I hesitated, but picked it up. It was Hugo.

"Ann? I need you."

I blanched. He could hear it.

"It's not what you think—" he said quickly.

I bit my lip. "Tell me," I said.

And he embarked on a long explanation, which I only half understood.

Well, look, it's like this. They—the Exchange Theater, his cultural center—were working on a housing project in the center of Brussels. Fighting urban decay—urban cancers, they called it—lovely old buildings bought up by multinationals and left to decay so they could be sold for vast profits, get the picture? But meanwhile, they turn into slums, Ann, and slums attract lowlife, and the lowlife forms into gangs, with knives and crack and so on, and then they take to the streets with the crack in their brains and the knives in their hands, for no great reason, just to create havoc, and the people in the city feel more and more unsafe, do you see?

Yes, I could see it very clearly.

Grist to the mill of the extreme right, he went on. Law and order, you know, zero tolerance and that sort of bullshit, exploit the feeling of insecurity of ordinary people, and they—the Exchange Theater—wanted to do something about that.

"It's people we care about, not money," I said. I'd read it somewhere.

Exactly, he said, that's why they wanted to do something about it, because the City Council wouldn't lift a finger.

"Aha, action?" I said, trying to sound interested.

Exactly, he said. Action.

"Sounds just like me," I said a bit cynically, but he let it pass. "What sort of action?" I asked next.

"Squat," he said.

Wow. Squat. Occupation. They were going to occupy a building. Very good. And what sort of building?

Well, he said, directly opposite the Exchange Theater there was a lovely old building, used to be a hotel, now a bit dilapidated (because it was owned by a Swedish finance company) but still worth converting to housing and shops. Now those damn Scandinavians wanted to turn it into offices at vast expense, but he didn't want to bore me with a lot of technicalities.

He was dead right. I nodded in agreement.

And they were going to occupy that building together

with an action group for inner urban renewal and socially responsible conversion of historically significant buildings.

I thought it was a good plan. I completely agreed with it, no question. But, to the point, Hugo. What do you need *me* for? What do I have to do?

"Photos," he said.

"Huh?"

"You must take photos of the event."

"Action photos? I don't know . . ."

"Don't carry on, Ann. I've seen your work, I think it's very good."

Where? Where had he seen photos of mine? I knew, really, but I wanted to hear it again.

In *Ear*, June last year.

That was right. I had taken photos, last year, of the open-air rock concert at school, and Bert had thought they were so good he'd sent them off to the editors of *Ear*. And they had actually published one of them.

Oh, that one. That was just an accident.

I actually thought it was very good. Very low light, spots among the trees, back-lit dancers, and in the foreground the overlit thick-lipped face of a guy drinking Stella from a cup.

"That was a fluke, Hugo. Lucky shot."

"*Please*, Ann?"

I muttered some more objections, for form's sake. Didn't he have any other photographers? They were all on holidays, he insisted. I bet. And what about that guy, the one with the loft in Ostend?

"Greg? He's in Kosovo."

Kosovo, for God's sake. I sighed. "Okay, then."

"I knew you'd do it!" he said. He sounded a bit too enthusiastic for my liking. But then, he was in show business after all. Ha!

"When?"

"Next Wednesday. Make sure you're here around seven-thirty. In the evening."

I felt a bit confused. I was relieved it wasn't "what I thought" (no big brother situation), and vaguely disillusioned because . . . for the same reason. And I was also quite pleased to finally have something to do.

Somebody needed me. At last. I didn't feel like a very useful person.

Long time no see

Of course, I was just a little scared, too. I was just about getting used to trains—two trips in one month!—but Brussels, that was unknown territory for me, a blank area on the map. In the almost empty dark green train (another dark green train) I studied, once again, the map Hugo'd faxed me, and checked, once again, my photo gear. I'd bought six rolls of black-and-white, Kodak T-Max 400 ISO. At a pinch, I could push that to 1600 if the light was really bad. I clicked my camera bag open, cleaned my lenses, and saw there was still a roll of film in my Nikon FA. One single exposure. Oh, yes, the photo of that photo.

At the exit of Central Station, I squinted into the low sun and started walking almost blindly. Between my lashes I kept an eye on the arrows marked on my faxed map. Cross wide street, left, then first right, across a large square on the left, straight ahead for a while, past a large building, cross a busy boulevard, and I should be there, Ort Street. Much to my own surprise, I got it right first go. Number 12 I was looking for . . . should be on this side . . . Then I heard my name being called from across the street. Hugo.

He gestured he'd be right there and kept talking briefly to a guy who looked like Yasser Arafat. Red-and-white-checked scarf and stubbly beard. They were standing in front of a building the size of a large apartment block. The ground floor was closed off with timber hoardings, which were covered in graffiti and half-torn posters stuck one over the other. Iam, De Puta Madre, Starflam, I even saw a shred of Mano Solo and a strip of Youssou N'Dour. I liked Youssou N'Dour. A few of the hoardings had been pulled down, exposing a decaying entrance with revolving doors, HOTEL CENTRAL in barely legible gold lettering above the entrance. So that was the hotel in question. Old gold. I looked up. An old, imposing facade, but badly flaking. A stylish old lady with lots of wrinkles.

Hugo and Arafat nodded at each other earnestly, slapped the cell phones on their belts like cowboys slapping their Colts: the action plan was ready, I guessed. Arafat went round the corner and disappeared up a side street. Hugo trotted across the road and hugged me hard.

"Hey, little monster, great to see you here. Exactly on time. We're just about ready to go."

"Who's Yasser Arafat?"

"Him? Oh, that's Pépé, the leader of the squatters. He's about to—"

He was interrupted by a howling like all the devils in hell. Half a dozen police vans swung round the corner and stopped, tires screaming. A small army of men in blue with Plexiglas shields and helmets jumped out, closed off the whole street, and formed a cordon across the hotel entrance. Their faces were grim, as if they were bit players in *Die Hard III*. The part of their lives. I swallowed. What sort of movie had I landed in this time? But Hugo kept his cool.

"Hm, they're quick today," he muttered. "Wait here a minute, Ann."

He went up to one of the officers and started talking to him. The officer shrugged, shook his head. Hugo laughed, causing the officer to poke him angrily in the chest. Almost automatically I got out my FA, clicked my 105mm lens on, and took a couple of shots. Suddenly I heard another camera clicking. Another photographer. Competition? Hadn't Hugo—?

The guy had an F3, autofocus. Top gear. What next?

He stopped clicking and gave me a grin.

"Hello, colleague," he said. "I'm Greg."

Greg? That Greg?

"Weren't you supposed to be in Kosovo?"

"Came back last night. Came straight on here. I'll do anything for Hugo. Or almost anything."

Him, too. How did Hugo do it? Nice-looking guy, this Greg. What a smile, what teeth. Cross between Brad Pitt and Michael Douglas. Complete with dimpled chin and steely blue eyes. But with blond curls. He looked approvingly at my lens.

"Nikon 105 without autofocus. Best lens in the world."

Yeah, right. I coughed. "Nice loft you've got. In Ostend."

"Oh, was that you? You're Anna?"

"Ann."

"Sorry. Ann. I like your hair."

"Thanks. I'm letting it grow."

"Good idea. . . . Listen, Ann, are you going inside, or will I?"

"What?"

"One of us is covering the outside, the other inside. That's what Hugo told me. Seems logical. So?"

"Oh . . . You go inside."

"Okay." He raced off round the corner, but came back right away. "You haven't got some spare film, have you?"

"Course." I tore my camera bag open, the Velcro ripping most satisfyingly. "Here."

"T-Max 400, perfect."

The right thing again. I began to feel better and better. With an apologetic grin, he took three rolls.

"No Kodak in Croatia."

"Croatia? I thought you were in Kosovo?"

"Yeah . . . there too, I mean, Croatia is on the way back. Croatia, that was the previous war, you know. Thanks a lot. If there's ever anything I can do for you—"

And he was gone, round the corner.

Anything he could ever do for me. I stood staring after him like a headless chicken. Then Hugo grabbed my shoulder.

"Hey, everything okay?"

Huh? Yeah, sure. And yes, I'd met Greg. He'd gone inside and . . .

"Perfect," said Hugo. "Perfect. Exactly the way I wanted it."

"How do you mean?"

"Come on, I'll show you."

He guided me inside "his" Exchange Theater, his cultural center. A large hall with lots of velvet, a crystal chandelier, and walls covered in graffiti. Hugo had a thing about contrasts. His office was on the first floor, on the street side. Through the large window we had a perfect view of the street and the hotel opposite. The Brussels police storm troopers stood in a semicircle round the entrance. Not even a rat would be able to slip past.

"What now?" I said. "Failure?"

Grinning, Hugo pointed at the next street corner. "Look," he said. "In that side street there's another entrance, and just as I had hoped, the police have forgotten about that for the moment. Pépé and his men are going in there right now, and . . . Oh, shit, they've woken up to it, I think. I just hope—"

The officer blew his whistle, and some twenty policemen stormed into the side street. Hugo grabbed his cell phone.

"Hello, Pépé? They've woken up to us, man. They're coming. How far have you gotten? What? Fantastic! *Great!*" He snapped his phone shut, radiant.

"They're inside, thirty of them."

"What next?"

"We've got an understanding with the police. They're under orders not to let anybody in, but they've promised us they'll leave the people inside the building alone. They thought nobody would get in, of course, but we've been too fast for them. Look, there's the officer again. Oh-oh, he doesn't look exactly happy. . . . Photos, Ann, photos!"

I focused on the officer, and as I pressed the shutter button, I burst out laughing. The guy looked as if he'd put his foot into a bucket of shit. I began to enjoy myself. Click, click, click.

"You know," said Hugo, "the police are really on our side. They would like nothing better than to see the inner city become livable again. But they're under orders from the mayor . . ."

"—and he doesn't want to do anything."

I began to understand a bit more, and to feel almost useful. We could see some movement in the hotel. Some windows were being opened, and squatters in colorful gear were appearing on the balconies. A large black banner was rolled out, two stories long. URBAN CANCER, it said in poisonously bright letters. I scanned the building, looking for Greg. Would three rolls of film be enough for him?

"Want some coffee? Sugar? Milk?" Hugo stood in front of the coffee machine in the passage and handed me a plastic cup. "Come on, I'll show you our HQ."

HQ was a half-dark room somewhere at the back where four or five people sat behind computer monitors, smoking cigarettes and chatting on telephones. Looked familiar. In the background three wide-screen TVs flickered, one showing a test pattern, one MTV, the third a local channel. A tall, thin guy in a *Laughing Cow* T-shirt came in carrying a big paper bag. "Crab roll anyone? Salad roll? Ham roll?" Hands went up behind the computer screens.

Hugo explained that they sent out press releases every hour, kept in touch with lawyers and with a few political parties who supported their action. Press releases? Lawyers? Political parties? Didn't sound like the Hugo I knew. I looked at him with new respect. This was obviously something different from dragging a few weird musicians out of the pub and pushing them onto a stage. This was a well prepared action, and socially responsible, too. So he could do that too, this Hugo. Perhaps you'll learn something about Real Life here, Ann!

And that's what I did, because the next few hours consisted mainly of waiting. I walked from the window to the coffee machine, from the coffee machine to HQ, and back to the window. "Just wait until something happens," Hugo'd said, but nothing did. In the street, more and more people arrived, lovely people, all sorts and colors. I took a photo, and I took another photo.

But somewhere in my head something started nagging again.

Hey, Anna, what do you think you're actually doing here?

It's Ann.

Whatever you say. But you know what I mean. Don't you?

Well, taking photos . . . Of an Important Political Event . . .

Bullshit, Ann! Why you, of all people?

Because I'm good at it, I suppose. Hugo asked me . . .

Exactly, Ann. Hugo! Wake up, child! Hugo? Michael? Marta? There was a question you wanted to ask Hugo, remember? Something about a certain letter, a letter you . . .

Okay, okay, I get the point!

I'd actually brought that letter, in the side pocket of my camera bag. Did I know why? Of course I did. Shit yes, did I know why! There was no getting away from it. Real Life, Ann. There were questions to be asked. Okay, then. What first?

I tried to think. Hugo'd got me here to take photos of his squatters' action. But he already had a photographer, Greg. Straight from Kosovo. A top photographer. Okay. Not being the star in this particular movie suited me fine. But would Hugo have asked me along as a spare? To sit on the reserve bench? Something wrong there. There had to be more to it. Or was there? Perhaps it *was* just that I really did take good photos, and that Hugo really did need two photographers? Mmm, yes . . .

But there was still that letter. I absolutely had to ask Hugo about Marta's letter. Did he know what was in it? Simple as that. For once, could I keep things simple? Okay, then. Right away, Ann. Now.

I went over to Hugo, who was on his cell phone again; the thing seemed to have grown onto his ear. He would have to have a chip implanted sooner or later.

"Hugo," I said, and he looked up absently, saying, "Yes?" and I asked him, Um . . . I asked him, Yes, well, what was supposed to happen to my photos, should they be printed right away and sent off?

"Oh, yes, sorry, Ann," he said. "There's a darkroom second door on the right. You'll find—"

Suddenly, shouting broke out in the street below, more sirens sounded, a few firecrackers went off, and we all dashed to the window. The street had filled up with people, it was like a football stadium. The police were obviously uneasy, and had called for reinforcements, who were now inching their way through the crowd with much noise and blowing of horns.

Evening was falling, and the blue flashing lights threw the surging mass into bright relief. Hugo said, "What are you waiting for, Ann? Photos, photos," and I clicked away again. There was some pushing and shoving here and there, and that provided some nice action shots. Not bad, I thought, not bad.

Hugo was worried the police would invade the building, despite their understanding, and he went down to the street to negotiate. I preferred staying up there. Safe behind my telephoto lens.

"You should really be down there," I suddenly heard beside me. It startled me. It was Greg. From Kosovo and/or Croatia.

"Get as close as possible to your subject. And when you think you're close enough, get closer."

"What?"

"Cartier-Bresson. The greatest photographer of this century."

"I think so, too."

"So what are you waiting for?"

I shrugged. What business was it of his? I could feel myself going rigid. Bitch.

He stayed beside me, looking down into the street. "Although it does look pretty good from here. And compressing your subjects with your telephoto lens works well. Gives great contrast—"

Hey, my friend, no need to lay it on that thick. If you think I'm a novice, I couldn't care. I'm only second string, you're the star here!

I glanced sideways. He looked pretty good in profile, too. I guessed he was around twenty-four, twenty-five.

"So," he said abruptly. "I'd better go and do some developing. Have you finished a roll?"

Two even.

"ISO?"

"800," I said, handing him my films, and he went off to the darkroom. I called after him, "Hey, how did you get out of there?"

"Through the door. The police won't let anybody in, but they will let you out."

"But now you can't go back in?"

"Oh, yes, I can."

He laughed briefly and disappeared.

I turned back abruptly and felt myself blushing violently. Bloody hell, Ann. I was carrying on like one of those mollusks from *Melrose Place*. Half fainting over a hunk with broad shoulders and white teeth, a whopping big telephoto lens and a sleeveless jacket with lots of pockets. "Sorry, Croatia, that was the previous war." Really? Boys and their toys. "Come on, girls, see how tough we are, look at us, please?" One has to have a glass of beer in his hands, another a fast motorbike between his legs, and another insists on playing tag at a front somewhere or other. Just like Michael. Who didn't take photos of mass graves and bloody corpses, oh no, he was just going to save the world. Or at least a piece of it. Just to prove how tough they are.

Hell, I was thinking about Michael again. And all because of this stupid Greg. Greg. What a name. Who's called Greg, for God's sake?

In short, it was on again: Anna—correction—Ann felt herself falling in love and was resisting vigorously.

Meanwhile, outside, Hugo was still conferring with the police chief, apparently successfully, because a couple of guys with pots and pans and big bags of bread were allowed to go in. I noticed there were lights on in the Hotel Central now. I clicked my 300mm onto my camera, focused on one of the balconies, and saw Yasser Arafat, aka Pépé, leaning over the cast iron railing. Nice image, a silhouette against the light on the balcony, and in the room swirling coiling clouds of smoke from a Rastafarian who was puffing away on a joint (or a Marlboro) below an incandescent globe, against a background of peeling wallpaper. I felt a bit of a voyeur, but that was all right this time. Click. I let my 300mm play over the facade some more, then over the crowd in the street, and suddenly my breath stopped.

I . . . no, it couldn't be. Impossible. I swung back a few yards, shit, shit, shit, my lens got out of control, people, faces, shoulders, coats, caps, hair flashed by super fast. Where was it, where had I seen it? Focus, Ann, keep it in focus . . . There! There! Shit, the focus ring, my fingers were all sweaty around the lens, I kept blinking, come on, Ann. There! Was that where it was? Was it really? No, it was someone else. Gone.

I'd dreamed it. I couldn't find it again. Exhausted, I lowered my camera and rubbed my eyes. I puffed. For just a moment, just the tiniest fraction of a microsecond, I'd thought I saw a head of long flax-blond hair.

Imagination, of course . . . I blinked again, looked at the crowd without the camera. There were at least ten blond girls, twenty, thirty . . . There were a million blond girls in the world. *Wake up, Ann!*

"Ah, Greg!" Coming up the stairs, Hugo nearly collided with Greg, emerging from the darkroom with the negatives.

"Any luck, my friend?"

"Very nice material, Hugo, very nice. Look, this one's good, and this one of Ann's, also very good . . ."

"You've got my complete confidence, amigo. Send them into the world."

Greg waved me over. "Come on, Ann."

I hesitated, looking at Hugo. "Hugo, shouldn't I stay here, in case something unexpected happens? Hugo?" But Hugo kept walking toward his office.

"Disappear into the darkness, my photographer friends," he called over his shoulder. "Send the world our images, in all shades of white and black and gray!"

The darkroom smelled nice. Of rotten eggs, citric acid, and ammonia.

"Wow, a Durst 300, with a color head!"

That moment I knew for certain: I wanted to do something with photography.

"We're not going to use that right now," said Greg. "Sit

down here." He pulled a second chair up to the computer in the other corner of the room.

"What? Aren't we going to print?"

"Welcome to the nineties," he grinned. A dark look from me, a shy grin from him. "Sorry. Come here, I'll show you."

Next to the computer stood a small negative holder. A film scanner. I'd seen them in *Foto 99*, but not in real life. He slid a strip of film into it, clicked with the mouse, and the photo appeared on the screen. It was the angry police chief. My photo. Greg laughed.

"Nice image. I can just see the headlines: 'Squatters Outwit Police.' What do you think? Brighten the face a bit, burn in a bit around the edges? That should make the graffiti in the background just legible . . . Okay with you?"

"Go ahead. You're the professional."

"It's your photo, Ann."

"I'm telling you, go ahead."

He right-clicked the mouse, swept the screen, brightening parts, darkening others, and my photo became almost perfect. Yes.

"Okaaay," he muttered quietly. "Now to just add the credits . . . Action Group Hotel Central, copyright Exchange Theater and Anna Br—"

"—Bracke," I finished and suddenly realized he knew my name. "Listen, how do you know my name?"

"Oh, from Hugo," he said casually. "Now let's send it off." A click on the telephone icon, the notice "sending . . ."

appeared on the screen, and my photo was on its way to the editors of the *Standard,* the *News, Morning,* and *Hello Brussels.* The wonders of technology. Welcome to the twenty-first century.

"That's number one," said Greg. "Now one of the squatters themselves . . ."

When he started moving the mouse about again, I put my hand over his. Felt good. But I kept my head on the business at hand.

"Wait a minute."

"What's the matter?"

"You know me."

"What do you mean, I know you?"

I shook my head. "You know more about me than you want to admit. You know more about—"

"About what? What do you mean, Ann? Of course I know you. Hugo is one of my closest friends, he's often told me about you. About you and your two—"

"—brothers, I suppose?"

"Yes, about you and your two brothers. Is that so strange?"

No, that wasn't so strange, but there was something else.

"Did you know I was going to be here?"

"What do you mean?"

"Hugo rang you in Kosovo, didn't you say?"

"Yes."

"How can that be? Isn't everything supposed to be destroyed in Kosovo?"

"Cell phone."

For a second I stared at him, dumbfounded. Yes, of course, a cell phone. Welcome to the nineties, Ann. Hello, darling? I'm ringing from the trenches. We're just about to attack, so I'll be a bit late tonight.

"Hey, Ann, what are you getting at?" Greg asked.

"And you came straight down? Just like that, just because Hugo asked? I mean, you leave all the world news behind just for a crummy bit of a report in Brussels?"

"Hey, hey, no, hang on. That's not how it was. My work there was finished, and Hugo knew that. He knew I'd be coming home around now. He just asked me if I could stop off in Brussels on the way back to Ostend. It happened to fit nicely—"

"When did Hugo ring you?"

"What is this, a cross-examination?"

"*Please?*"

"Well, let me think. I was in the car . . . day before yesterday, or was it the day before—"

"You were in the car?"

"Yes. Ah, yes, now I remember. The day before yesterday it was, I was already in Croatia, the Dalmatian coast—"

A sudden knock on the door. "Hey there, knights of the telephoto lens! Can I come in, or is there a magic ritual going on?" Hugo's voice.

"Come in," Greg called.

The door opened a crack, and Hugo's head appeared. "Greg, can you come here a minute? A job."

Greg jumped up and briefly put his hand over mine. "Be

right back, *Inspector Morse,*" he said with a smile. "And, by the way, I think you take bloody good photos."

The door closed, and I was by myself in the half dark. Inspector Morse, Inspector Morse!

But his story could well be right, I thought. When Hugo rang me last week, he genuinely didn't know yet if Greg would be available. And so he had asked me. And when it turned out that Greg would be available after all, he hadn't canceled, because two photographers are better than one. I was a good second. A supporting role, but a big supporting role, Ann. ("Bloody good photos," Greg had said, and for just a second I blushed.) But all the same.

But all the same. (That other story again. All the time!) Greg knew me, and he knew my two brothers. Didn't necessarily mean anything. Hugo was his friend and could have told him all sorts of things, but it all seemed too much of a coincidence. To be honest, I hadn't thought much about the Michael business the past two weeks (hadn't *wanted* to think about it much, Ann, admit it), but now it was all there again, and it fitted so exactly it made me feel scared. Greg knew him, he knew my two brothers, and at the very moment Hugo rang him, he was happily driving through Croatia, the Dalmatian coast, to be precise. That might be the normal route for journalists returning home from the front in Kosovo (should check that), but still, but still . . .

I had turned my chair back to the computer and was mechanically sliding the strip of black-and-white film back and forth in the scanner, and the day seemed to speed past on the computer screen. I saw the policemen around the Hotel Central, Hugo with the police chief, the graffiti on the hoardings, Yasser Arafat with red-and-white-checked scarf, and then suddenly Michael and Jonas. The image stopped moving. Oh, no. There they were again. Complete with the tear between them.

That one photo. Of course, it was on the same roll of film. Had Greg noticed it when he developed the film? Not important, Ann. Not now. I stared at the screen, cursing silently. The only photo I had taken at the seaside. One single bloody photo. And even then . . . A photo of a photo isn't a real photo, is it?

I ran my finger along the tear on the screen, just as I had two weeks ago over the real tear in the real paper. Suddenly I had an idea.

"And why not?" I muttered. I put my hand on the mouse the way Greg had shown me, clicked on the eraser icon, and with slow, careful sweeps on the screen I digitally made the tear invisible. It took forever, and it felt good and bad.

That tear was years old, and I felt it like a tear right through my body. Did I think I could fix it with a simple digital operation? Something not right there. On the other hand, what was it that Daniel Devolder had told me in the train about the magic of photography? "The strength of a photo lies in what is absent." Hell, I thought. All that absence! All those years! Years of absence, Anna. For years you've missed your brothers, first because they were never there, absent, then because they were dead, absent . . . Time it all stopped. Jonas is dead, but Michael . . . And why *shouldn't* you hope, Anna? Why not? God, how I longed for a big brother.

Then there was another, very soft, knock on the dark-room door.

"Come in, Hugo," I said, without looking up.

The door swung open, and a beam of white light split the darkness. Hugo stepped into the room and looked at me, clearly embarrassed.

"Anna, there's someone here to see you."

I got up slowly. I already knew who it was. Hugo stood aside, and a woman appeared in the doorway. A woman with long, flaxen hair. Beautiful, against the light.

"Hello, Marta," I said.

"Hello, Anna," she said. "Long time no see."

Marta and I

There we stand, as if petrified, me in the half dark, Marta and Hugo against that bright yellow backlight. Silhouettes. It takes a long time before anyone moves. Then Marta steps toward me, takes my hand. My hand is sweaty, but I don't pull it back. I can barely see her eyes, but notice her looking at something over my shoulder. The computer screen. Then she turns abruptly toward Hugo, nods at him. Hugo understands, gives me a quick look, and leaves, pulling the door shut.

It takes a while for my eyes to adjust to the half dark again, but Marta doesn't let go of my hand. We stand for a short while, then she gently pushes me toward the computer. We sit down, Marta and I, in front of that screen, with Michael and Jonas.

"I know that photo," she says. "Nineteen-eighty-eight, isn't it?"

I nod.

"I didn't know Michael then. I was still living with my parents, in Rijeka, Slovenia, and studying modern history at the university in Ljubljana. Capital of Slovenia. Officially, we were still part of Yugoslavia, even though Tito was long since dead. Tito *was* Yugoslavia, you know."

Yes, sure, modern history, I think.

"And Michael?" I ask. I'm startled by my own voice. She smiles quickly, without looking at me.

"In 1989 I got a scholarship to study in Italy. Florence. I stayed with my aunt Jelena. I met Michael on a trip with other students. He's so awkward, starts blushing and stuttering the minute he sees me. So serious, too"—she lets go of my hand and briefly touches the screen, just above Michael's eyes—"with that high forehead of his, and that permanent frown. . . . But that same week he invites me out to his apartment in Fiesole. He's dead nervous, makes a mess of the wine and the glasses and all that, but it's a lovely evening, and we sit out on his terrace till deep into the night, watching the lights in the town below, the tower of the Signoria and the dome of the cathedral, and then, very late, we go back in and I see that photo on the wall. 'Who's that?' I ask. 'That's me, and that's my brother,' he points out. I didn't even know he had a brother. 'Stepbrother, anyway,' he mutters and starts talking to me about Belgium and Jonas. And about how it doesn't matter whether you're full brothers, or step or half brothers, or whatever—"

Suddenly, Marta turns toward me, and I can see her eyes.

"As long as you feel the bond," she says. Those eyes of hers are incredibly blue. The lightest blue you can imagine, I can see it even in the darkness of the darkroom. "That's how Michael put it, 'As long as you feel the bond.' Michael and Jonas had a bond like that, I could see that right away." Her finger keeps moving over the screen, pauses between Michael and Jonas and briefly follows the direction of the tear that's no longer there. I start trembling. How can she possibly know about the tear? She can't. Not important anyway, Ann, not now.

"The moment I saw him in that photo, before I even met him, I loved Jonas. He was totally different from Michael, I realized that immediately. Handsome, too. And he released things in Michael, how shall I put it . . . Whenever Michael talked about Jonas, he became . . . more uninhibited, more boyish, do you understand? And that frown disappeared from his forehead. No, Jonas was a very special person . . . A real brother, for me, too."

I have to swallow. Then she looks at me again, asks, "How old were you when that photo was made? Five? Six?"

I nod.

"I was there," I say.

"There?"

I point at the screen. "Look here. See their eyes? They're not looking into the lens, they're looking at me. I was standing next to my father when he took the photo."

She laughs, and I see tears in her eyes.

"It's such a lovely photo," she says, shaking her head. "So much warmth. Michael took it with him wherever we went. We've moved often, as you know, and every time that photo had to come."

"And now?" I ask.

"What?"

"And now? Where's that photo now?"

She doesn't answer right away. I hold my breath. Then she says, "On the wall at my place."

At her place? As if she's talking about an heirloom! But then Michael must be . . .

But it's as if she suddenly realizes she's said something terrible. She shakes her head vigorously and takes hold of both my hands, squeezing them. Hard. She bends toward me and looks straight into my eyes.

"No," she says. "No, Anna, it's not what you think. He's *alive*, your brother! Believe me. I'm sorry if I—"

"Michael's alive?"

"Yes."

"But?"

"Not now, Anna. It's a long story. But he's alive, believe me. Please!"

I shut my eyes, breathing deeply. Michael's alive. Michael's alive. I keep repeating it in my head, I try to understand it, but I can't, I can't. Impossible to say if I'm glad. I simply don't know what's happening to me.

I hear a chair being moved. I open my eyes, and Marta's standing before me. I haven't been dreaming.

"Anna?" she says.

"Yes?"

"In my letter . . . um . . ."

"What about it?"

"I asked if you could do something important for me."

"And?"

"Will you still do it?"

"What do I have to do?"

"Come with me. I'll explain the rest on the way."

"Sure," I say.

She opens the darkroom door; bright yellow light makes

me blink. Like an automaton I walk after her. Michael's alive.

Hugo was standing at the big window in his office, looking down on the street.

"Is it going all right, Hugo?"

"Wonderfully."

We went to stand next to him. It was like watching a movie. The dark blue police vans, the shiny helmets, the flashing lights, the increasing crowds of people, the TV crews with their spotlights, the Hotel Central lit up festively, the balconies, the windows—it was so beautiful, it was like a New Year's Eve celebration in midsummer. Braziers glowed everywhere, there was a smell of fried *merguez* sausages and roasting lamb. Long tables had been placed in the middle of the street, soup, beer and wine were being served, and here and there musicians had set up with guitars and accordions. The whole neighborhood had come out into the street, and it looked as if half of Brussels had joined in. The *Die Hard* policemen had suddenly become your friendly neighborhood cops. Flowers had been put in their buttonholes, they had pushed up the visors of their helmets and were drinking beer and lighting cigarettes, laughing. A film, Ann, and not even a bit part for you. But that didn't matter, not anymore.

"Where's Greg?" asked Marta.

"Gone home."

Marta nodded. "Good. Time for us to get going, too, don't you think? Have you got the keys?"

"Here." Hugo went to his desk and gave her a car key.

"Where is it?"

"Outside the back entrance. I'll come down with you."

He went ahead of us through a maze of steps and cellars and opened a metal door. The night air was fresh, and the street quiet. Snatches of music and shouting echoed against the buildings.

"The dark blue Ford, over there," he pointed. Marta nodded.

"Thanks for everything, Hugo. Take care." She kissed him on the cheek and walked to the car. I didn't know which way to look, and had started to follow Marta when Hugo stopped me.

"Hey, you forgot this." My camera bag. I slung it over my shoulder. Felt good.

"Thanks," I said.

"Hey, Ann . . ."

"Yes?"

"Sorry." He looked me in the eyes—the first time for a long while. "I couldn't do anything else."

That's all right, Hugo, that's all right, but I really have to be off now. He stopped me again.

"One more thing," he said. "Just before he left, Greg told me your photos were really very good. Very, very good, he said, and if I ever needed photos, I should think of you."

I stood on my toes and kissed him quickly on the cheek.

"I hate you," I said. "But you're really rather nice, Hugo." And I followed Marta.

Marta steered the Ford through the almost deserted streets of the inner city. "I've often been here, with Michael," she said. "Going to embassies, for papers and that sort of thing." She pointed to the right. "That's where the Croatian embassy is these days . . . Round the corner the Bosnian, and Serb . . . officially Yugoslav, but for me Yugoslavia is still the Federation, you know. Now where is that bypass road? Ah, now I know where I am."

Her words came through to me as in a dream. I watched us driving up a wide boulevard, diving into a tunnel and emerging again, passing a large church and leaving the city in the direction of the freeway. A blue direction sign: Paris 297 km, Ostend 101 km, Valenciennes 123 km.

"Where actually are we going?"

"To the coast."

"The coast? Not Ostend?"

She smiled apologetically. "Sorry, Anna."

For God's sake, Ostend! Ostend again. And who were we going to see? I knew just about half of Ostend. My father, Devolder, Greg . . . Hang on—Greg? Now I could see it. Greg had just come from Kosovo, or was it Croatia? ("Croatia, that was the previous war.")

"Greg?"

Marta nodded. "I came with Greg in the car."

Shit! I should've known. "From Zagreb?"

"Yes. Hugo knew I wanted to come to Belgium. He rang Greg in Kosovo, and Greg picked me up on his way back."

"When was that? How long have you been here?"

"We arrived in Ostend the day before yesterday. I'm staying at Greg's place."

I thought for a bit.

"And how did Hugo know you wanted to come here?"

"I rang him early in July, to tell him I wanted to come to Belgium."

"What for?"

She sighed. "Those letters to you were . . . yes, well, they were not such a good idea. I've talked about it with Hugo, on the phone. We should've thought about it more carefully. But everything went so fast, in Rovinj, and we both had the same instant reaction to what happened: to let you know something. A sign of life, something . . ."

"But don't forget the red felt pen, eh? *Don't say anything to your parents, Anna!*"

"I know, I know. I told you, we didn't think it through carefully enough. And then Hugo stupidly sent his letter to Holsbeek, so of course Irina started to suspect something was going on."

Yeah, I thought, where else should he have sent it? But she was right about Mom suspecting something. Her absences, those midnight phone calls . . . Come to think of it, I should call her; here we were, merrily driving to the coast, and Mom knew nothing about anything.

Marta shook her head. "Don't worry. Hugo's warned her it could be pretty late, and you'd stay the night in Brussels."

Don't worry, *don't worry!* Shit, what next? Letters I wasn't supposed to have received, messages I had to keep quiet about, a half-failed trip to Ostend, and then two weeks of silence, while behind my back the phone lines between Ostend, Brussels, Zagreb, and Kosovo ran hot. Next I am lured to Brussels on false pretenses, and now here I am in a car with the sister-in-law we'd thought was dead, on our way to the coast, where no doubt another pleasant surprise is waiting for me. Don't worry, Anna! Bloody hell, what a mess!

Gloomily I turned to the side window, and for a while I sat, cursing silently, staring at the road, at the light poles and the white lines sliding past. *Prisoner of the white lines.*

Suddenly the engine roared as Marta accelerated to pass a camper, only to jump on the brakes immediately to avoid a tractor-trailer that cut in front us. I was scared witless, my hands started to sweat on my knees, Marta flashed the headlights, cursed in Serbo-Croatian, accelerated again, and passed the truck, loudly blowing the horn. My heart beat in my throat.

"Hey, do you have to drive so fast?" I shouted. "Are the Mafia after you or something?"

"Sorry, Anna."

"Ann!" I said angrily. "It's Ann, damn you!"

"Sorry, Ann."

"Answer me! Are the Mafia after you or something? You drive like you're in a gangster film. What's all this about? All this secrecy, what's going on?"

Marta raised her eyebrows, then slowed down.

"Better like this?"

"Mmm," I grunted, rubbing my hands dry on my knees.

"Listen," she said. She was trying to make her voice sound calm, as if she were talking to a difficult child, which only made me more angry. "Listen, I come from a country that's at war, I can't help it—"

"War? Come on, Croatia isn't Kosovo! In Croatia, things are quiet, Hugo told me so himself."

"Oh, *yes?* Well, I happen to live there! I really do know what I'm talking about. In the whole of the Balkans, nobody is free from war."

"Well, this isn't the Balkans, this is Belgium!"

"Listen, if you know it all, you can get out now, d'you hear? Do you think I'm enjoying all this?"

"So tell me what's going on. It's driving me mad!"

But she shook her head obstinately. "No," she said. "When we're in Ostend, I'll tell you the whole story. Right now . . . I can't."

"Get lost, then!" I shrugged and stared moodily through the windshield. What was the point of it all, anyway?

Silence for a while, then I heard Marta cough.

"All right," she said. "There's one thing I'll tell you, but promise me you won't ask any more until we're there, okay?"

"All right by me," I grumbled.

"Have you ever heard of Arkan?"

Arkan? That rang a bell. I'd read something recently, in a magazine or somewhere. But I could be wrong.

"Gangster, drug smuggler, assassin, mass murderer, war criminal, you name it. But he is also a respectable businessman, owner of FC Obilic, for example, a Serb soccer club. They've sold players to Club Bruges, for instance—"

That was it. That's what I'd read about that guy.

"His real name is Zeljko Raznjatovic, but he is better known as Arkan—Serbian for 'wildcat'—commander of the notorious Tiger Brigade, an extreme Serb nationalist private militia. Those Tigers are really just a murder squad. During the war in Croatia and Bosnia, and now again in Kosovo, they've carried out hundreds of ethnic cleansings, under the approving eye of Radovan Karadzic, Ratko Mladic, and now Slobodan Milosevic himself. An extremely dangerous man, this Arkan."

"Yes, and?"

"Wait. In the seventies, Arkan joined the SBD, the Yugoslav State Security Organization. Tito had developed a number of extremely efficient secret service organizations. One of their tasks was to keep an eye on Yugoslav emigrant communities in Western Europe and to 'neutralize' possible opponents of the regime. For such dirty assignments, they often employed criminals, who in return for their 'contributions' were allowed to organize their criminal activities without interference. Arkan was one of those criminals/secret agents, and carried on the SBD traditions enthusiastically. He murders by order, faithfully carries out ethnic cleansings ordered from Belgrade—like recently in Kosovo—and meanwhile he quietly develops any Mafia-style activity you can imagine: illegal arms dealing, drug trafficking, smuggling cigarettes, coffee, cars. . . . And of course he has his men everywhere to keep an eye on things, all over Western Europe, even in Brussels. He actually knows Belgium pretty well, he's been in jail here, in Verviers. He's been in the Bijlmer jail in Amsterdam, too."

"Yes, but—"

"What I want to make clear to you, Ann, is that I have good reasons for all this secrecy. I have felt really unsafe, you know, for more than two years now. Even when I'm in Ostend or Brussels."

I still didn't really get it. I'd seen *The Godfather,* of course, but . . .

"But what on earth have you or Michael got to do with that Arkan? Jee-zus, Marta, that guy doesn't keep every single Croatian or Slovene in Europe under surveillance, does he?"

"Not me. Nor Michael, directly. But Michael's father does."

Swallow. Michael's father. Mom's first husband. Totally forgot. What was his name again? Goran—?

"Goran Lupovic. A commander in the Yugoslav People's Army. One of the original Serb hard-liners after the collapse of the Federation. Took part in the first fighting for Krajina in 1990, together with—guess who? Arkan's Tigers. Promoted to major. Since then, he's been seen constantly in the entourage of Karadzic, Mladic, and . . . Arkan. Probably involved in the slaughter at Bijeljina, at Brcko and Srebrenica."

"Enough, enough." I'd gone cold. Michael's father, a war criminal? A mass murderer? "But—" I stammered. "Michael hadn't had any contact with his father, had he, since his parents separated? I mean—"

Marta hesitated. "Not quite right. Michael did." She stopped abruptly.

"What? What did Michael do?" I suddenly remembered a passage in her letter: *terrible things have happened.*

"Please, Ann, no more questions now, you promised. I really have to tell you the whole story, all of it, later, when we're there." She looked at me, and I saw she could barely control her tears. I nodded, briefly touched her hand. She smiled gratefully.

"Okay, then," I said. "But where is Michael now? Sorry . . ."

She shook her head, quickly wiped away a tear, swallowed, and stared straight ahead.

"Are you beginning to understand why I have to be so secretive? Perhaps it was a bit exaggerated, perhaps I'm a bit paranoid, but I felt safer in the anonymous crowds of Brussels. Our meeting wouldn't be so obvious. Even your mother wouldn't think it suspicious. That business in Brussels was the perfect cover."

"Mm." I nodded and thought of something else. I tried to imagine how I would have reacted if I'd suddenly just got a phone call from Ostend. Probably total panic, paralysis. While now I was in the boat and had to row, whether I liked it or not.

A blue traffic sign slid past. Ghent.

"A good half hour," said Marta.

"Ostend forty-five miles," I read. A good half hour, yes.

Marta and Michael

A brick facade. HUNGARIA in large, peeling letters. I'd seen this before, but in daylight. I looked over my shoulder. The lighthouse, blue-and-white striped, lit up eerily. A flash, a beam of light swinging round. Like a searchlight in a concentration camp. I shivered.

The lift seemed even noisier than last time, but that may have just been my imagination. I could feel the rattling in my stomach. Third floor. Marta raised the grating as quietly as she could and put a finger over her lips. We walked on tiptoe.

A pile of blankets on the couch started to move.

"Marta? Ann? Is that you?" The words were muffled, but I recognized the voice.

"Greg?"

He sat up, grinning. "Of course, Greg. I live here, remember."

I took a step forward and bumped into something.

"Ssh!" they both said, pointing to the corner. There was a cot there.

Like a robot, I went and bent over it. At first I couldn't see anything but a little heap of blankets that breathed, I mean they moved up and down. Then I saw, just above the edge of the blanket, a thick bunch of black, curly hair, two small round cheeks, velvety eyelashes, and a little bit of a nose. I jerked round.

"Marta? Is this? I mean, is this your—?"

"That is Michael," she said.

For a moment, I thought I'd misunderstood. "Michael?" But she nodded. "Michael?"

"Michael junior, our child, Michael's and mine."

My fingers clutched the edge of the cot like the railing of a ship. Kate Winslet in *Titanic*. Everything was spinning around me. Marta came and held my shoulders.

"Isn't he beautiful?"

I nodded speechlessly.

Then there was a soft cough behind us. "If you ladies don't mind, I'd like to catch up on some sleep. I've had a busy time, you know."

"Sorry, Greg, you're right," said Marta.

"The bed is made. You'll find everything you need there." Greg waved in the direction of the sleeping corner, turned on his other side and was still.

"What do you think?" said Marta. "I'm dead tired."

"Me, too."

I had one more look at the cot. The child slept on as if nothing was going on.

I woke to the smell of fresh coffee. I looked around, dazed. Sunlight came streaming in through the windows. On the couch a crumpled-up blanket. Oh, yes, Greg. The loft. Marta? She stood by the cot, watching me.

"He's still asleep. Would you like coffee?"

"Where's Greg?"

"Gone to buy some rolls."

She went into the kitchen, then came and sat on the edge of the bed with a cup of coffee. I took a sip and pulled a face. Phew, it was strong!

"Don't you like it?"

"Yes, I do. What's the time?"

"Early." She ran her hand through my hair. "You've cut it."

"I'm letting it grow again."

"Good, you've got lovely hair."

"So have you."

She smiled. "I'm so glad to see you, Ann."

"Me too, Marta, me too."

She gave me a kiss; I put my arm round her shoulders and hugged her. Felt good, very good.

Then she broke out of our embrace, raised her shoulders—no, just her right shoulder—and said, "Shall I tell you everything now, while he's still asleep?"

Suddenly, I was wide awake. "Yes, yes," I nodded, and stepped out of bed.

We sat on the couch by the window, and Marta told her story. She spoke softly, rapidly, almost constantly gazing out of the big window overlooking the sea. Every now and then she took a quick look at the cot.

"September '96 was a busy month for both of us," she began. "Michael was in Sarajevo, and I was traveling through Bosnia to do a report on antipersonnel mines. We called each other a couple of times a week. I remember Michael getting quite worked up about that Dutroux child sex scandal, which all of Belgium seemed to be in a state about. I could understand him, you know, it was a terrible business, but I thought we really had no shortage of child murderers ourselves in Bosnia. Perhaps you think I'm being cynical, Ann?"

I shook my head. Not at all. We had discussed this in our history course: Was Hitler worse than Stalin? Is a hundred dead worse than one? You can't draw up a league table of horrors.

She nodded vaguely, thought for a while. "Anyway. I'd finished up near Foca, a border town about sixty miles from Sarajevo. I'd made contact with a French de-mining crew of the SFOR."

"SFOR? What's that?"

"The NATO peacekeeping force. We'd arranged that I'd go with them the next day, to see their work. That evening Michael arrived from Sarajevo, for a few days' break. He looked exhausted. His work, I thought. He'd been working with those kids from the war for two years without a break. That's a terribly long time. Most people doing that sort of work don't last more than six months."

"And his music? Did he still play?"

"He played the clarinet for the kids . . . Folk songs. No time for study, of course. Michael was really obsessed with his work, he loved those children as if they were his own."

I bit my lip. "Macho Michael, who absolutely had to go and save the world," I'd sneered not all that long ago.

Marta was silent for a bit, then picked up the thread of her story again. "The next morning, October 3, 1996, we left very early. I introduced Michael to the two Frenchmen, Louis and Yannick, nice guys. Two more people came in the Land Rover: Mohammed, a young Muslim who'd lost a foot in a mine explosion—I wanted to photograph him in the mine-field—and his girlfriend, a girl of about twenty. Her name was Mirjana. On the way she was joking about her name, because her favorite group was Nirvana. Mirjana, Nirvana, you know. We were going to drive out to a field about twelve miles southwest of Foca.

"Michael was terribly irritable that morning, and when I asked him what was wrong, he snapped at me so rudely it scared me. He didn't say another word all the way. Let things cool, I thought. I was pretty tense myself, and you could end up having a fight before you knew where you were. I started chatting with Yannick, asking him about various types of mines and leaving Michael in peace. In retrospect, it would have been better if I hadn't. If I'd told him then why I was so tense that morning, everything would probably have turned out differently."

"So why were you so nervous?"

"I'd done a pregnancy test that morning."

"No!" I stared at her open-mouthed and pointed to the cot.

Marta nodded with a sad smile. "He was two on April 15."

"And . . . and Michael?"

"I'd planned to tell him that morning, but decided to put it off for a bit because he was in such a state. I wanted to wait for the right moment. Ah, the right moment!" She had trouble controlling the trembling of her voice, swallowed hard. "Just after that, it happened. Foca was some distance behind us, we were driving into a deserted village, most of the houses in ruins. Michael had been looking out of the window in an agitated way for some time, as if he was looking for something. I hadn't the foggiest idea what it could be, because as far as I knew, he'd never been in that area before. But when we reached the first houses, he suddenly shouted, 'Stop! Stop!' Louis was driving. He looked at Michael in surprise and braked. Michael jumped from the car, gesturing wildly that we should drive on. I couldn't understand it. I jumped out, too, but he pushed me back and screamed, 'Get back in! You've got nothing to do with this!' Of course I refused, asking for an explanation, but he was as stubborn as a mule. I'd never seen him like that, and I didn't know what to do. I couldn't leave him alone, he was so distressed. Finally, I told Louis he should drive on. 'We'll follow you on foot,' I said. That was fine, Louis said, their minefield was only a couple of miles farther on. He told me the way to go. 'But stay on the road, pretty girl, there are still lots of mines in the fields!' He blew me a kiss; the Land Rover took off and disappeared among the ruined houses. I went up to Michael. 'Are you finally going to tell me—?' At that moment, we heard an enormously loud bang.

"'Oh, no! The Land Rover!' Michael shouted, and we started running. Around a corner, we saw it, just outside the village. Somehow or other, it had veered off the road and hit a mine. It was on fire. The hood was completely gone. We could not see the passengers through the smoke and fire. Michael was faster than me, he was already close to the wreck, ten yards, five, I don't know, when suddenly there was another explosion. The gas tank, I suppose. The force of the explosion threw me to the ground, I rolled onto my front, my mouth in the sand. Wreckage was flying around, pieces of metal and rubber, and there was noise everywhere. And a stench: burned tires, and sulfur, particularly sulfur, I remember it clearly. As if someone had struck ten million matches at once. After a while the noise stopped, but the stench remained. I scrambled up and saw Michael lying in the middle of the road. On his back, close to the jeep, or what was left of it. I screamed, I think. But he was moving. I ran to him and helped him up. He was bleeding from some abrasions but nodded at me shakily. 'Okay, okay,' he said. I screamed, cried, yelled all sorts of things at him, but he didn't react. I shook him by the arm. He pointed at his ears, gesturing helplessly. 'I can't hear you, I can't hear you,' he said. He was deaf."

I nodded. Like Tom Hanks in *Saving Private Ryan*. "What about the people in the Land Rover?"

Marta looked at me, shrugged. She got up, went to the window, and looked out. The sun was already high, it was going to be another beautiful day.

"The weather was just like this, that day," said Marta. She turned her back to the window, the one with the crack in the glass, and leaned against the windowsill.

"I had a cell phone, but it had stayed in the car. Weird, really. There were four dead people in that car, and I thought about that phone! There was nothing for it but to walk back to Foca. It was nearly evening when we got there. I was worried about Michael. I'd been talking to him all the time, but he stayed deaf. Literally. There were an unusual number of soldiers in the streets of Foca, and dark blue Yugoslav army jeeps. Serbs, that is. They seemed terribly tense. We went straight to our guest house, and I asked what had happened. 'Don't you know?' asked the landlady. 'The SFOR have arrested a Serb major today, a war criminal they say!' 'Who?' I asked. 'A man called Lupovic.' I turned to Michael, but of course he hadn't heard anything. I pulled his arm and dragged him up to our room. 'Michael!' I screamed into his ear. 'They've arrested—' But Michael desperately pointed at his ears. I grabbed a piece of paper and wrote, *They've arrested your father.* I pushed the note under his eyes. He read it and nodded."

Marta was silent again. Her eyes gleamed. Tears? Beyond the window the sea gleamed, too. Salty, gleaming water. A huge expanse. Then Marta continued.

"That look of his, Ann! The way his eyes looked. So blank, so hopeless! It was as if all life had gone from his eyes. And he just sat there, his hands over his ears, with those dead eyes. And that very moment I understood what had happened. What he had done."

I didn't yet. I stammered, "You don't mean—? Marta, he didn't—? Not really?"

But she nodded. Yes, really, she nodded. And then she said it: "Michael had denounced his own father to the SFOR."

"As a war criminal?"

"Yes. I had known for some time that he was working on it. He didn't say much about it, but I knew he was trying to track down his father. And as I told you last night, I knew that Goran Lupovic was to be found in the immediate entourage of Mladic and Karadzic, and that those men were carefully guarded. Still are. But apparently Michael had got on their trail, and he had also discovered that his father had committed war crimes."

"Srebrenica?"

She shook her head. "Those were only suspicions. Suspected of involvement in the slaughter at Srebrenica and so on, remember. You can't accuse someone on the basis of suspicions. But Michael had found proof of something else. Other crimes."

"What sort of crimes?"

"De-mining."

"De-mining?"

There was something mechanical about her voice now. As if she was saying something into a tape recorder. Something that would have to be used as evidence before the tribunal in The Hague or something.

"The Serbs in Bosnia had developed a unique technique for clearing minefields. They would take a number of Muslims prisoner, transport them to the minefield in trucks, and then force them to walk together, abreast in a long line, through the minefield. Anyone who refused was shot. And those who didn't refuse . . . Well, some survived. And a number of those survivors have testified—and their testimony was confirmed by independent sources, as they say—that Major Lupovic regularly used that technique, between 1994 and 1996, with great enthusiasm." She took a quick look at the cot. "But Michael only told me that much later."

She thought.

"It was also only much later that I understood why Michael wanted to get out of the Land Rover in exactly that spot. One of the survivors was the father of a little boy Michael had looked after for UNICEF, and this boy had told him that there had been one of those mine-clearing operations in a field just outside that village, and that the operation had been led by Michael's father. I suppose Michael wanted to see the place with his own eyes."

"Why?"

"Don't know. They say a murderer always returns to the scene of his crime . . . Perhaps Michael wanted to do that in his father's place. Something like that."

"So, really, Michael's father saved your lives."

She looked up, surprised. Then she smiled cynically. "I hadn't looked at it quite like that."

Just then, we heard the lift gate open downstairs. The big cage juddered into motion, and a moment later we saw a large white paper bag rise above the floor, followed by Greg's head, his teeth bare in a smile like a Colgate commercial.

Then the rest of him followed. He was carrying the bag on his head like an African woman balancing a water jug. He stepped out swaying his hips, bowed smoothly, and with a flourish offered us the paper bag.

"Fresh rolls, *bwana*."

Marta and I looked at each other, restrained ourselves for a moment, then burst out laughing. Greg looked hurt.

"And to think I woke the baker up especially for you!"

The bundle in the cot stirred. Marta started burbling at Michael Junior in Serbo-Croatian. She picked him up and proudly sat him on her arm. She wiped the tears of laughter out of her eyes; the little one rubbed the sleep out of his eyes and looked at us, puzzled, and we all roared with laughter. The child burst into tears and pressed his face against her breast. Marta kissed him and stroked his black curls.

"Strange sight, isn't it?" I said. "Your blond hair and his black curls."

"Yes, he really didn't get that black from me," she laughed. "Well, Greg, I'm ready for one of those rolls. And so's Michael, I think,"

"And me," I said.

"And coffee, I suppose, and fruit juice, and cheese, and ham and milk . . . the works?" Greg said, and Marta and I looked at him approvingly. Well, why not?

"Coming up, ladies. And everything free of hormones and dioxin. Guaranteed!"

Greg disappeared into the kitchen, and soon it was like a holiday. We pushed the table near the couch and breakfasted with a view of the sea. Little Michael ate and drank and knocked his cup of milk over and laughed and wanted more chocolate and pushed his finger in the jam jar and we all laughed, yes, that's how simple life could be. A child woke up, and the problems of the world had to give way.

"I've even taught him a few words of Dutch," said Marta. "Listen . . . Michael, say 'opa.'"

"*Oppa!*" Michael trumpeted.

"Lovely. Now say 'oma.'"

"*Ommaa!*"

Bravo, bravo, applause all round, and Michael Junior crowed with pleasure. And immediately I understood something. Another bit. I was really learning a lot lately.

"Hey, Marta?" I asked. "Why did you teach him the two Dutch words for grandparents?"

"That's what I'm here for, aren't I?"

"Just as I thought."

"Michael wanted to . . . But I'd better finish my story first. You'll find it easier to understand then."

"You know what," said Greg. "I'll go for a walk on the beach with our young friend here for a while. So you can have some peace."

"Good idea," said Marta.

Greg sat on his heels and tapped his shoulder. "Michael! Come on! Shoulder ride!" Whooping, Michael stormed toward Greg and started climbing onto him. Greg got up, and Michael shouted with fear and delight. Smiling, Marta waved them out.

"They're best friends," I said. "And in such a short time."

"Yes, Greg is terrific."

"Isn't he?"

Marta looked at me meaningfully. "Oh? Really?"

"Okay, okay," I grinned, blushing.

"So you're not cross with him anymore?"

"Cross? What for?"

"You know, the plot? Hugo and he really fooled you, didn't they?"

I shrugged. "No, not anymore. Anyway—"

"Anyway what?"

"No, nothing, forget it." I had suddenly thought of something, but I kept it to myself. And perhaps I was wrong anyway. "Tell," I said.

"It's strange," she said. "I actually hate all this hide-and-seek, particularly when friends are concerned, but I've had to do it so often in the last few years I've got . . . But I'd better tell you everything. Where was I? Ah, yes . . ."

She had gotten up and was now walking around the room, opening drawers, lifting stacks of papers, and rummaging in the fruit bowl.

"What are you looking for?"

"It doesn't happen often," she said, "but all of a sudden I desperately want a cigarette, and I think I saw a . . . Ah, here."

She lit a Marlboro, took a quick puff, and looked at me guiltily. Then she sat down on the couch, folding her legs under her.

"That same evening we left Foca. Escaped, really. And two days later we were in Zagreb, with few problems on the way. Fortunately, Michael and I both have an international passport. In Zagreb, we stayed with my friend Sanja."

"The address on your letter."

"That's her. Sanja Paljutek. A very good friend. When I'm in Zagreb, I always stay with her. The next day I took Michael to a doctor. It was worse than we had thought. Irreversible damage to the eardrum."

"But do you know for sure? I mean . . . Is there really nothing that can be done?"

Marta pulled a face and threw her half-smoked cigarette out of the window.

"It's so hard to say with that sort of thing. Honestly, Ann, I don't know. He wouldn't seek a second opinion. I think, if he had himself examined properly in a good hospital . . . The last time I saw him, he could hear a tiny bit in his right ear, he said. I don't know, Ann." She sighed, then continued.

"After Zagreb, we lived in Italy for a time. In Fiesole. He still knew some people there from his student days, and they discreetly organized a small apartment for us. But, as I said, something had died in Michael. He refused to go to a hospital and be assessed. They can do so much these days, I said. But he wouldn't hear of it. Ha!" She laughed grimly at her own unintended joke. "He was out a lot, wandering for hours through the hills. And in the flat he locked himself in his room. His voice sounded stranger and stranger."

"So how did you communicate?"

"I wrote everything down. He answered orally. But finally there wasn't a lot to say anymore. Then, a few weeks later, we read in the paper that we'd both died in an accident with a Land Rover in Bosnia. Weird, reading the news of your own death in a paper! He didn't say anything. He grabbed a piece of paper and wrote angrily, *I'm dead. Good. Keep it that way.*"

She picked an apple from the fruit bowl and put it back again.

"Of course, there was also the problem of our safety—I've explained that to you already—and it suited us quite well that Arkan and Goran's Serb friends thought we were dead. That was when I decided to 'keep it that way,' but with all of you I still feel it was unforgivable. I thought of you a lot. I could imagine what the news would do to you, and I'm sure Michael thought about it long and hard, too, and that it hurt him as much, but the few times he was prepared to talk about it, he kept repeating the same thing: He wanted to be dead. Dead to the world. Dead to everybody. I respected that. And when he disappeared not long after, I had no choice."

"What do you mean, disappeared?"

"A few days after the news item in the papers, he left the apartment very early, as usual. I took the bus to Florence, to see my aunt Jelena. I went to see her often. She's the only one who knows about everything."

"And Sanja?"

"Sanja?" Marta laughed, hesitated. Then she grabbed her bag and produced a passport. "Here, have a look."

My mouth fell open. I read, *Sanja Paljutek, nationality Croatian, born in Split, thirty-one years old, profession journalist . . .* with Marta's photo next to it.

"So Sanja . . ."

"Sanja doesn't exist. *I'm* Sanja."

"How did you get this?"

She shrugged. "Aunt Jelena is married to a diplomat. Michael's got one, too. Officially, his name is now Michele Boccelli, born in Milan, doctor of sociology, living in Fiesole. If you lie, you should lie close to the truth."

"That aunt of yours must be good at it."

"At what?"

"Lying. Mom rings her regularly."

"I know, I know," sighed Marta. "Oh, it's all horrible, Ann. I'm so sick of it."

I took her hand for a moment. "Go on," I said softly.

"When I came home that evening, all his CDs were in a heap in the middle of the living room floor. Smashed into a thousand pieces, with his boots or with a hammer, I don't know. Those things are pretty solid, I'm told. There was a yellow note on top of the bits. 'Sorry, darling. I am dead.'"

"Did he know you were pregnant then?"

"Of course," she sighed. "Of course he knew. He went away in February. I was seven months gone then."

"And even that didn't stop him?"

"No."

"What a bastard!" I let slip.

But she reacted vehemently. "Don't ever say that, Ann!

Don't ever say that! If anyone has the right to judge, it's me. And I don't judge. So, please, shut up!"

I lowered my eyes, stared at my hands on the tabletop. They were shaking. Marta was right. I had no right to speak.

Then suddenly her hands were on mine. I looked up. She smiled.

"Sorry, Ann," she said.

"No, no, it's me . . . sorry . . . you," I stuttered in a kind of Swahili, and suddenly felt my eyes filling with tears. I couldn't help it. Never thought I had so many tears. I'd cried a few times the last few weeks, but these tears were different. Marta got up slowly, walked round the table, and put her arms around my shaking shoulders. She rocked me in her arms and hushed me the way she had her child just before, and that felt so good. It was a long time before I finished crying.

Then I asked, "Why now, Marta? Why now, after all this time?"

Her face turned serious again. The story went on, but her voice sounded much less mechanical now.

"He's come back," she said.

I was startled. "Michael?"

She nodded. "Your brother."

Her husband. "When?"

"A few days after I'd bumped into Hugo in Rovinj. My aunt has a summer house in Rovinj, and Michael knew that. One morning, he was suddenly standing at the door. Just like that. He looked, shall we say, reasonably okay . . . Reasonably calm. He didn't stay long, you know. We had breakfast together, and when the little one woke up, we went for a walk along the wharf."

"Is he still—?"

"Deaf? Oh, yes. And he still wants to stay deaf, the idiot. Refuses any examination, any treatment, while I know almost for sure . . . 'This isn't a matter for doctors, Marta,' he told me once, and I think I know what he meant. We sat on a bench and I told him—via yellow notes, of course—about meeting Hugo. It didn't seem to penetrate at first, but then he suddenly said, in his weird voice, 'I want my parents to see the child.' I thought I hadn't understood him properly, but he repeated his words, every syllable. Would I do that for him, really, he meant it. I stared at him for a long time, and then I said, 'Michael'—I articulated every letter of every word, and he was hanging on my lips, almost literally—'Michael, don't you want to be dead anymore?'"

Be dead . . . Why can't the bastard just stay dead! I thought back to my first reaction to Hugo's letter. Oh, God! Listen to Marta, Ann, listen to Marta. She knows a few things about death and life . . . How all that works . . .

But Marta suddenly seemed far away.

"Marta? Marta?"

"Yes?"

"Michael?"

"Oh, yes . . . oh, yes . . ." As if she was waking from a dream. "He looked at me for a long time. He just stood there, not moving. And finally he said, 'No, Marta, I don't want to be dead anymore. I want to live.'"

"And his sign of life, that's . . ."

She nodded, staring dreamily out to the beach. "His son."

I followed her glance. Her son walked somewhere on the beach. Michael's son. My nephew. And Greg.

"And then?"

Marta shrugged. "He disappeared again. That was in the beginning of July. That's when I rang Hugo to tell him I wanted to come to Belgium. You know the rest."

I nodded. I knew what followed. But there was one other thing I wanted to know. One thing she hadn't told me yet. "There is something else."

"What?"

"You told me there are only three people who know what's going on: Hugo, Greg, and your aunt Jelena."

"Yes. So?"

"There is someone else."

"Oh, yes? Like who?"

"While you and Greg were in Brussels last night, who was looking after little Michael?"

She frowned at me, a faint smile playing around her lips. "You tell me."

"You'd never have engaged a strange baby-sitter. You're too suspicious. So it must have been someone you knew, someone you trusted. And you don't know that many people in Ostend. Could it, for instance, have been someone who used to know Jonas quite well and so got to know Michael and Hugo too, and who was really interested in your articles when I happened to meet him a few weeks ago?"

She shot me an approving glance. "Daniel Devolder. Clever, Ann, very clever."

I flushed, but I agreed that it was pretty clever, to be honest. I cleared my throat and asked, "Has he known all along?"

Marta shook her head and looked at me quizzically. "No," she said. "He only knew for certain after you told him."

"Me?"

"Yes, you. That evening after the Mano Solo concert, remember? Hugo had been trying to reach him for days, but failed because Daniel was in the middle of moving house. Just before the concert, Hugo managed to whisper a few words to him, but Daniel could only be certain when you told him about my letter and my articles later that evening."

Well, hell! It was *me* who told Devolder! And it would have to be that drunken evening, with all that business with Bert. Oh, no. Now I really felt myself blushing, and Marta burst out laughing.

"Yes, I've heard all about that evening," she laughed. But then she was serious again.

"You know," she said, "I think he has suspected for a long time, but he's never let on. Anyway, he helped us a lot, over all those years."

"How?"

"Money."

"Money?"

"We've never been well off, Michael and I. UNICEF paid Michael, and I wrote the occasional article for a paper, but that didn't add up to much. We traveled a lot, and Michael was too proud to ask Holsbeek for money. Every now and then, Daniel sent us some money. 'Consider it a loan,' he said. And after our . . . accident, well, then we were really hard up."

"But after your accident, he must have known then?"

"He sent it to my aunt, and later to Sanja. He didn't ask questions. 'For that project in the former Yugoslavia,' he wrote to my aunt."

I leaned back. So, Devolder. Not that it made any difference, but I was glad I knew.

I looked up. Marta was back at the window, her hands raised to her eyes like binoculars. Now it was my turn.

"And now?" I asked. "Something important?"

"Yes," she sighed. I already knew what it was.

"*Ommaa* and *Oppaa*?"

She nodded slowly. Went on looking out to sea. And then I said, feeling cowardly, but at least honest, "But, Marta, you could do this yourself, couldn't you?"

"No," she said. "Honestly, Ann. I don't dare. I don't dare look them in the face."

"They'll be pleased—"

"No, really, I don't dare. Not yet."

"Okay," I said, and she nodded gratefully.

And then Marta went down to the beach to fetch the child. Michael's child.

And I got on the phone. Revolting device, the phone, but I managed. I keyed in both their numbers, I talked to both of them, and they both came.

epilogue

Dear Doc . . .

Ostend, Thursday

Dear Doc,

Do you think it odd that I'm writing to you? I do. Especially seeing I'm just a couple of floors away from you. Letters are usually something you write to people far away. But you're probably looking at the same things I'm looking at right now: the almost deserted beach, the sea, the pier, a catamaran approaching the harbor in a cloud of foam . . . If you haven't drawn the curtains, the sun shines into your room, too, causing all sorts of strange reflections on the wallpaper. And can you see, like me, those three small figures walking on the sand, near the breakwater?

I'm not much of a letter writer, really, but I suddenly felt the need to sort today's events—and the rest!—quietly in my head, because my head's in a real mess (again!). Perhaps I'll manage by writing. In a drawer of Dad's desk I found a new packet of writing paper (nice, a fresh pack of paper), and I started off. Hope it'll work.

It is now Thursday, July 15, nearly eight o'clock in the evening, and I'm in my father's apartment (6D). I'm on my own. My parents have gone down to the beach with their grandchild. The little one is mad about the beach. If it was up to him, he'd sleep there, I think. Their grandchild. It's almost unbelievable. After all those years of death and loss, there is a sign of life.

Okay. The facts. I'll start with today, round about midday. What happened before that you already know, I assume? Anyway, that's what I'll assume. (Not easy, you know, writing to you like this. I know *roughly* what you knew or know, but every now and then I'm uncertain. Yes, well, listen, if I write things you already know, just skip them. I can't help it, after all, it's you people who've made things so complicated. Not me.)

Okay, today, then, about noon. Marta and me in the loft. Greg's playing with little Michael on the beach. Marta's finished her story and says, "Call your parents, tell them to come." And she leaves me alone, says she's going to get Michael from the beach. I do as she asks, pick up the phone, and dial the Holsbeek number. Mom's beside herself, shouts something into the receiver, and hurls it down. I can hear the gravel on the drive crunching under the smoking tires of her car. While I dial Dad's number, she's already tearing along the freeway at ninety-five, I'm sure. Our house in Holsbeek is hardly over a mile from the freeway entrance. I just hope she doesn't get stuck in a traffic jam, she'd explode. Dad's answering machine is on. I hate those things, but I leave a message anyway. Please call me back at this number, it's urgent. I stand by the window, biting my fingernails. What more can I do? Nothing. The beach is getting busy. Where's Marta now? Greg and the child? I can't make anything out—just hordes of stupid tourists with sunshades and beach umbrellas. I dial Dad's number again. Answering machine again. I stand by the window again, bite another bit off my fingernails. Shit, what's keeping Marta? It's taking so long. Every five minutes, I look at the clock. Any minute, Mom will be here, and you'll see . . . that very moment Marta will walk in with the child, and then—I don't dare think of it! I'm about to try calling Dad again, but the phone rings before I can. "Hello? Anna?" Phew, Dad. At last. "Listen, Dad—" He reacts a bit slowly, that's what he's like, as if things don't penetrate immediately. Then he says, "I'm coming." Sigh. I hang up. Then I hear the elevator—Marta, with little Michael. Greg isn't with them.

"Are they coming?" she asks.

I tell her they're on their way.

She nods. "I'll be off, then."

"Hey," I grip her arm. "You really don't want to be here?"

"No," she says, a bit embarrassed. "I don't dare. Not yet." She gives me a kiss. "Thanks," she says.

Then she gives Michael a cuddle, explains a few things to him (I suppose—I understand practically nothing of it), and she's gone. The child is standing in the middle of the room, looking at me with large eyes. As if he feels something special is going to happen. Do something, Ann.

"Hey, Michael, let's play a game?" He doesn't understand me, of course, keeps looking at me with those huge dark eyes. I think, Serbo-Croatian, think of something in Serbo-Croatian! I rack my brain, this is coming from very far down, but then I find something. "Hey, Michael . . . Game? *Igra?*

Igra?" His face lights up. "*Daaa!*" he shouts, and I frantically look for a toy. Unlikely that Greg has a Lego collection, but then I spot a toy car in the fruit bowl. "Auto!" I call, and for a while we *vroom-vroom* happily on the coffee table. Then he says something, and then something else, all the time looking at me with those big questioning eyes. I break into a sweat. What to do? And later, with my parents here, what's it going to be like? I am the go-between, I am the key person, I have to make it happen. No way back.

When Marta had explained what the "something important" was she wanted me to do for her, I'd thought, big deal! Introduce a child to his grandparents, what's so hard about that? (Why don't you do it yourself? I thought, but if Marta couldn't or didn't dare, who was I to judge?) "'Course I'll do that for you, Marta. No problem, if that's all." *I had no idea!*

Exhausted, I sink down on the couch, my T-shirt drenched in sweat. Ten minutes! Ten minutes I've been on my own with the child, and I'm stressed out. And this isn't even what it's all about. It's all about what's still to come: my parents, their questions, the past, the confrontation, a conversation, a long-awaited meeting . . . all things I'm really good at! But I *must* make it happen. You're in charge, Ann. Michael pulls at my arm. "Ann! Auto! Auto!" he screeches. Yes. Yes, I'm coming. *Vroom-vroom.*

Then a real car stops in the street, tires screaming. I walk to the window, my heart thudding. "Mom, here!" I wave. At the same time, I see Dad coming round the corner. On foot. Out of breath, by the looks of him. "Dad! On the left behind the gate there's a freight elevator. Third floor!" I take a deep breath. Okay, Ann, here we go!

The elevator came rattling up, and it was like an invasion. The two of them stormed into the loft, straight at me—Anna, what, how, where, why—but before I got a chance to panic or utter a single word, there was a "vroom-vroom" from behind the couch. Dad and Mom suddenly went very still.

"Michael?" I say. Michael appears, smiling broadly, waving the toy car.

"Ann! Auto! Vroom-vroom!"

"Michael, look. This is Oma and Opa . . . Ommaa and Oppaa . . ."

He frowns, as if he has to think about this, but then his face clears. "Ommaa! Oppaa!" and he runs to them.

My parents spread their arms, get down on their knees, and hug the child. Michael puts up with it all, giggling under their kisses and cuddles. Mom starts talking to him in Serbo-Croatian, which pleases him even more. Dad finds his handkerchief and blows his nose loudly. Little Michael gets a fright at first, but then screams with laughter. He shouts something I can't understand. "More!" Mom translates with a laugh. "You've got to do it again, Pierre!" Dad laughs through his tears and blows his nose again, even louder than before, and Michael claps his hands, and Mom laughs and cries. And me, I just stand there, watching it all happening, and I blub like a child. I turn away and go to the kitchen, and I keep on crying. God, the amount I've cried the last few hours, or days, I don't know anymore.

Suddenly, I feel a hand on my shoulder. It's Dad. His eyes are red, too.

"Come," he says. "We have to talk."

"Oh, yes, we do."

Mom was sitting at the table, Michael on her lap. She'd given him a banana, and he was totally focused on eating it. That child does absolutely everything with total concentration, he's dynamite! Dad and I joined them at the table and then came the questions. Plenty of them. I answered as best I could, and was surprised at how calm I was and how easily we talked. Do you remember how smoothly our conversation went that evening at your place? But then we had your Italian wine to ease things along. Now, there was no wine. Just my parents, the child, and me. And I managed it all.

What I told them was roughly the story Marta had told, and they hung on every word. In an odd way, I enjoyed myself. For years, they had kept all sorts of things from me, had kept me out of their story (although I must admit that for years I hadn't wanted to know). Now the roles were reversed, and I had a secret story I'd been keeping from them. At first they were uncomfortable with this new situation, but gradually the awkwardness drained away, for all three of us, and it was no longer important who had kept what from whom and why, because there was an end to all that. We could just talk, my parents and I, uncensored—and that was important. No more red felt pen.

(For exactly the same reason, I no longer care who kept what from *me* during the last few weeks—you, Hugo, Greg, or Marta or whoever—or what plots you did or didn't hatch, and under what pretense I was lured away somewhere. I really don't give a damn any longer! Seeing my parents with their grandchild, I know for certain there are more important things!)

Little Michael was getting tired and started to whine. Mom went to put him down to sleep, and that was quite a performance with a song and a story, Dad looking on tenderly.

"Shush," Mom said from the cot. "He's asleep."

Mom came back over on tiptoe and had just sat down when the elevator started rattling. We were startled. Someone was coming up. Greg, I thought, it must be Greg. I started to explain about the person who lived in the loft, this photographer who'd just returned from Kosovo and so on, but then my voice faltered, because I saw a head of blond hair appear. Very long blond hair—no, I wasn't dreaming. The elevator kept coming up, and there she was, all of her.

Marta.

For one moment, an eternity, she stood motionless behind the grille. Then she pushed it open and slowly walked toward us. She ran her fingers through her hair, which was all blown by the sea wind, stopped, and asked, "Michael?"

"He's asleep," said Mom, and she got up, and so did Dad, and everybody embraced everybody—confusion and delight, and tears, lots of tears once more—my God, Doc, I didn't know what to think, where to look, what to do. I think

I ran back to that kitchen and cried all over again, but it was so good, and it felt so warm inside me.

Soon after, we all sat round the table by the window. I'd got drinks from the fridge, ice tea and Perrier and Mexican beer, and once more there were lots of questions. Marta talked. About Michael. About herself and her son. Mom asked some of those real mother-in-law-questions about the birth and breast-feeding and so on, and Marta laughed, like any proud young mother.

Then Dad asked, "And Michael?"

"I don't know, but—" said Marta.

"Where is he now?"

"I don't know, Pierre. I told you! For the last two years, I've never known where he was."

"Sorry. Go on," said Dad.

"I don't know . . . but this time I really think he'll be back soon." She said it with her eyes closed, as if she was pronouncing some sort of spell. Or a prayer, for all I know. Dad lifted one eyebrow—I hadn't seen him so lively for a long time.

"How can you be so sure?"

Marta opened her eyes and looked at him hard. "I am not at all sure, Pierre, I have no certainty at all. But the last time I saw him, I had a very strong feeling that something had changed . . . in him. There was life in his eyes again."

Once upon a time, Dad would have reacted cynically to this—"A feeling? Life in his eyes? Bah!"—but now he didn't. He looked thoughtfully at Marta, and nodded.

"And Goran?" asked Mom, a little fearfully. Michael's father, her first husband. Marta shrugged (I knew that gesture).

"What do you think? Very soon after his arrest, he was set free again. In exchange for a couple of Bosnian prisoners. They couldn't do a thing to him, he was protected."

"But what about The Hague? The International Tribunal? Wasn't there a charge against him?"

"Apparently not officially. But that may change soon."

"How?"

"Kosovo," said Marta. And she launched into a lengthy explanation about Kosovo, Milosevic's strategy, the carefully planned ethnic cleansing, the role of NATO, and the weak-kneed policies of America and England. "Kosovo was one bloodbath too many," she said. "Until now, the international community—America and England, that is—have tolerated Milosevic for the sake of stability in the Balkans and that sort of bullshit. But they couldn't tolerate the brutalities he perpetrated in Kosovo without seriously losing face. So they started bombing—"

"And so Milosevic is under real pressure now," Mom nodded.

"Right. But don't have any illusions. Heads will roll, for sure, but they won't be Milosevic's, Karadzic's, or Mladic's, the brains behind the ethnic cleansing. Those guys are too big, too powerful. No, if any head's going to roll, it will belong to one of the subordinates. The subordinates are dumb bastards who carry out the orders of the smart bastards, and when the fortunes of war change, they're the first ones to cop the blame. And they're bloody well aware of it, those subordinates, they're not as dumb as all that."

"Goran?" Mom asked.

"Perhaps," Marta said evasively. "But I was really thinking of—"

"Arkan?" I said.

Marta nodded. "And when we're talking about Arkan, we get back to us again, I mean Michael and me."

Mom shifted to the edge of her chair. Tell us, tell us, her eyes said. Marta put her hands flat on the table, her fingers spread.

"After Kosovo, Arkan is really feeling the heat. He has no more options. Milosevic washes his hands of him, and Arkan knows what that means. Several of his colleagues have already been found with bullets in their heads. On the other side, there's the West, and the West is after his hide. So Arkan changes direction. He abandons his Yugoslav paymasters and tries to make contact with the West, in Belgium among other places. He wants to come to an agreement with our legal authorities; according to some sources, he's actually in Belgium right now. That can only mean one thing—he's looking for a deal."

"What sort of a deal?"

"Simple. Arrest me, but give me protection. In return, I cooperate with you, supply information."

"Yes, but," Dad interrupted irritably, "what's all this Arkan business got to do with you? Or rather, what have you got to do with all this Arkan business?"

"Don't you understand, Pierre? Arkan is Goran's friend, Michael has accused Goran, so Michael and I go into hiding to escape from Arkan and his secret murder squad. But now, after Kosovo, Arkan's position has become very shaky, and he's got other things to worry about. Like saving his skin! And so Michael and I can afford to feel a lot safer, you see?"

"And that's why you could come to Belgium now?" I said.

"Yes. We still have to be very careful, but I felt I could chance it. Before this, I was too afraid, for myself and for Michael. And I didn't want to put any of you in danger, either."

Dad shook his head in disgust. "What a bloody awful mess! I don't even know who to be angry with. I mean, who's to blame for the whole shambles? For two whole years I've had to be without my grandson. For two whole years I haven't seen my son. And now I find out it's all because of some mad war criminal who just happens to be a friend of my son's father? And that the whole bloody thing has to do with international politics, balance of power, protection of criminals, and hypocritical strategies? Bloody hell, I just don't get it, Marta, I can't begin to understand!"

Mom took his hand. "Hey, Pierre," she said gently. "Why don't you just blame me? Once upon a time I was married to Goran, he's my boy's father. If Michael is involved in this, it's because of me, isn't it?"

I'd sat there thinking about this for quite a while, Doc, and I'd been watching Mom constantly. My mother was once the wife of a war criminal, a brutal murderer! I just couldn't understand how she could accept that so calmly. Had she already known what sort of man he was? And how much more had she found out later, after they separated? But suddenly it occurred to me that Mom knew exactly who Marta had meant when she said she didn't want to put any of us in danger—it was she, after all, who was Goran Lupovic's ex-wife!

Stunned, Dad looked at her. He wanted to swear, swear hard, I could see it, but he didn't.

"Oh, no, Irina, no," he said quietly. "Don't say that. Not that. I married you because I loved you, it was as simple as that. And I love Michael as my own son, no matter who his father is, no matter where he comes from, you know that. It was like that from the start, and nothing about that has changed."

"Nothing, Pierre?" she asked, sounding incredulous, even a tiny bit amused—or was that my imagination?

He hesitated, taken aback, then said, "Shall we discuss that later, Irina? I think there are more urgent matters right now."

Mama smiled agreement. "Good. But don't wait too long." She squeezed his hand, then let go of it. God, how I loved my mother right then! "And now, Marta?" she asked. "What are you going to do now? You're going back, I assume?"

Marta nodded. "Greg's leaving for Romania in a few days, on an assignment. I can go with him as far as Zagreb."

"Greg?"

"The photographer. He lives here," I blurted out. And immediately felt myself blushing violently. Mom raised her eyebrows.

"Greg?" she asked. "Anna?"

"Leave it," I said, annoyed. She laughed.

Dad pushed his chair back noisily and stretched. "Fresh air," he said. "That's what I need." He pointed to the window. "Anybody feel like a stroll? It's such a lovely day."

We all agreed with that. Soon after, Michael Junior woke up, and we went down to the beach together. I'd hoped Greg would turn up, but he was obviously keeping a discreet distance. Ah, well. Anyway, the sight of my parents with their grandchild was definitely worth seeing. More than that. I was really happy, Doc, on the beach there.

I'm almost through with my story. It's getting dark here. I've switched on a desk lamp. The horizon is a riot of color, lots of orange and fiery red, with a few dark gray stripes of cloud running through it. The sun doesn't seem to want to set, and I sympathize. The beach is getting a bluish tinge, like in that painting on your wall. I can't see those three little figures anymore. I expect they'll be home soon.

We've got ourselves organized, Marta and us. Mom and I are going to stay a few days, at Dad's, and Dad's pleased. Little Michael can sleep here tonight, he really wants to, with "Ommaa and Oppaa," and Marta's pleased. She's staying at

Greg's. Early tomorrow she's coming here for breakfast, and we're all pleased.

I'm feeling weird, Doc. My fingers are cramping, I haven't written so much in ages. I just found something by Mano Solo in my father's CD collection, a song about the sea and the beach, about screeching cormorants, about the tides and the wind on your bare skin. About leaving and returning, about life and death, and how good it feels to really return. It's called "Je reviens."

I'm glad I've written all this down. I would have loved to drop in on you this evening, but I'm far too tired. Is it okay if I call in tomorrow, after breakfast?

I can hear the elevator buzzing, the cables creak, the door clicks open. They're here.

See you tomorrow, Doc.

Much love from

Anna